Major Benjy

Major Benjy

A Mapp and Lucia novel

Guy Fraser-Sampson

First published 2013 by Elliott and Thompson Limited
27 John Street, London WC1N 2BX
www.eandtbooks.com

ISBN: 978-1-908739-70-4

Text © Guy Fraser-Sampson 2013. Originally published by Troubadour Publishing, 2008.

9 8 7 6 5 4 3 2 1

A CIP catalogue record for this book is available from the British Library.

Typeset by Marie Doherty
Printed and bound by CPI Group (UK) Ltd, Croydon, CR0 4YY

This edition is not for sale in the United States of America.

Chapter 1

The picturesque town of Tilling perches confidently on a rocky outcrop that once jutted proudly out to sea, making it an ideal setting for a constant game of hide-and-seek between smugglers and customs men. Alas, the natural harbour which had been the town's *raison d'être* silted up, and the English Channel gradually retreated, leaving behind only salt marshes and colonies of vociferous gulls. Despite these vicissitudes of history, however, Tilling remains a popular and attractive place of residence for ladies and gentlemen of refined tastes, and its landmarks, such as the Landgate, the gun platform and the delightful church, offer ready subjects for what they typically refer to in self-deprecating fashion as their 'daubs'.

Had one been standing on top of the church tower one spring morning, one would have seen the blackness of the night sky beginning to acquire a distinctly purplish tinge over the Kentish marshes to the east, which could perhaps have been conveyed by some rather daring sponging with cobalt violet, before turning rapidly into a pinkish-grey mistiness, which would in all conscience have required talent of Turneresque proportions to portray, talents far beyond those even of candidates considered by the Tilling hanging committee. However, even while their hesitant hands had been reaching for the permanent magenta, the pure pale sunlight for which Tilling is justly famous would have spread rapidly across the landscape below like a giant rug being unfurled, and the town would have acquired the appearance by which it was instantly recognisable from any number of paintings. Apart, that is, from those of Irene Coles, universally known as Quaint Irene, who, while being Tilling's only acknowledged professional artist, seemed to perceive Tilling somewhat differently from the mere mortals around her, and whose views of the High Street could inexplicably involve large numbers of naked people dancing around a burning town hall while winged and clawed ghoulies, some of which might bear an amazing though surely accidental resemblance to various worthy Tilling residents, hovered and screeched overhead.

Sadly, though, nobody was standing on the church tower to admire this artistic kaleidoscope unfolding, since it was generally recognised that polite society in Tilling did not rise before nine, at which time one might decently draw back one's curtains and consume a hearty breakfast. It was, however, understood and accepted that Miss Mapp would rise well before this point, since she was known to favour the early morning as her 'thinking time', when she would sit dreamily in the window of the garden room at Mallards with a finger resting across her chin and a faraway expression on her face, surely too dreamily for anyone to think that she might be observing the manner and time of her neighbours' houses coming to life.

This morning the famous Tilling sunshine beat persistently against a bedroom window upon which Miss Mapp's glassily unseeing gaze had been resting for a good hour or so, and filtered into the room through the cracks in the shutters, casting a ladder of light and shade on the countenance of a middle-aged man lying in bed and becoming slowly and somewhat reluctantly acquainted with the happy morn.

Major Benjamin Flint, late of His Majesty's Indian Army, was apt to be in poor spirits first thing in the morning, and could frequently be heard berating his servant should his kippers be cold or his porridge lumpy. On such occasions he would confide to his friends that he was 'not quite the thing' that morning, and would hint darkly at recurrent and mysterious diseases of tropical origin. His friends would naturally commiserate most sympathetically with an officer who had been forced to do such violence to his long-term health in the service of King and country. Yet as soon as he moved on they would conjecture amongst themselves that the good major's ailment probably had more to do with prolonged exposure to Bombay gin than to the city of the same name.

Major Benjy, as he was known to his friends, lay in that halfway state between sleep and wakefulness, when one is fully conscious only of a headache and trying to come to terms with the enormity of getting out of bed, while being somewhat preoccupied with thoughts of something one has forgotten and really should have remembered. With a heartfelt groan he swung two hairy legs out of bed, felt for his slippers, and then opened the shutters. This proved to be something of a mistake as the pure Tilling sunlight struck him squarely in the face and he uttered a little cry and tottered backwards, sitting down again heavily on the bed. From her vantage point Miss Mapp heard the cry and stored it away tidily in that part of her mind which was reserved for the fermenting of solicitous enquiries after an individual's well-being which could be delivered quizzically, though in a kind, neighbourly fashion, during the morning's shopping.

Major Benjy's second attempt at embracing the day was rather more successful than the first and some moments later found him sitting at the breakfast table, which Sarah, his servant, seemed quite inexplicably to have neglected to lay that morning, and staring fixedly at his newspaper. Fixed though his gaze might be, his nostrils twitched, at first with puzzlement and then with mounting rage. Where his olfactory receptors might reasonably have expected to encounter the aroma of toast, kippers, bacon or coffee, they met none. The conclusion was inescapable: his breakfast was not ready, not even in the course of preparation, and so his brave attempt at coming downstairs without even the benefit of aspirin or bicarbonate of soda had been in vain. He drew an ample breath and shouted 'Quai-Hai!' at the top of his voice, though he knew it was likely to hurt. It did.

Framed in the window of her garden room, Miss Mapp allowed a knowing smile to flit briefly across her face. At much the same time the Major, still attempting to focus on his newspaper, happened to open it at the page of classified advertisements and in that moment there came upon him the awful realisation of what it was that he had forgotten but really ought to have remembered. Sarah, having given notice a month previously when he had occasion to exchange sharp words with her about his kippers, had left the day before, and his increasingly desperate efforts in recent days to find a replacement through the columns of the *Tilling Gazette* had proved fruitless. There was no Sarah to make his bed or tidy his room. There was no Sarah patiently to retrieve his golf clubs from the various corners into which he flung them after losing half a crown on the eighteenth green to the Padre. Worse still, infinitely worse, there was no Sarah to cook his breakfast. He gave a hollow groan, dropped the newspaper on to the bare table and went dejectedly in search of Alka-Seltzer.

Miss Mapp, by contrast, decided that she had probably been seen at her thoughtful best for quite long enough for one day, and busied herself with her preparations for her daily shopping trip. Shopping for oneself may be thought of as something of an eccentricity when one has a servant, but to refer to Tilling's morning *passeggiata* as 'shopping' would be akin to describing Wagner's Ring cycle as light musical entertainment. First it was an opportunity to keep oneself abreast of Tilling developments, and here there was a whole ritual of exchanges to be observed, starting with the hopeful query 'Any news?', not forgetting the ejaculatory 'No!' of feigned disbelief and secret delight at each new disclosure. For the 'news' referred to was not of the variety that could be found in any newspaper, except perhaps occasionally in the *Tilling Gazette*. There was a world beyond Tilling to be sure, but no true Tillingite deigned to acknowledge it. Their world was bounded by the stone walls of the original cinque port. Even Tilling new town could be regarded as *terra incognita*.

Second, it was an opportunity to display a new outfit, and never more so than now, at what could almost credibly be called the start of the summer season. Shopping in the crude sense in which that word was used outside Tilling society, the actual purchase of comestibles, came a long way third. Miss Mapp would typically content herself with one or two choice items which would not weigh down her basket too heavily while she was standing talking, and leave the real business of stocking the house to her servant, Withers. Fridays were the only exception to this rule. On the fifth day God had created the great creatures of the sea and winged birds, but for Miss Mapp it was when she sallied forth, her weekly books of account in her basket, to indulge in numerous highly enjoyable arguments with the local tradesmen.

Happily this was not a Friday and so she would be able to devote herself entirely to the welfare of her fellow Tillingites. She donned hat and gloves in front of the hall mirror and stepped into West Street with her usual rolling gait. The first house on the left was that of the Major, standing opposite what had until quite recently been the home of the late Captain Puffin. It had been the scene of scandal when the Major and the Captain were understood to have fought a duel over the matter of her womanly affections, and she was careful to deny the story afresh every time there seemed any danger of the incident being forgotten.

Her shortest path to Twistevant's, the greengrocer, lay undeniably to the right, but she hesitated and turned left instead, to knock a trifle imperiously at the Major's front door. There was what sounded suspiciously like some swearing from the innermost depths, and then the door was opened abruptly by the Major himself with a peremptory 'Yes?'. It was unfortunate that a combination of a bad hangover and no breakfast should have made the Major forgetful. It was doubly unfortunate that what he should have forgotten were his trousers.

Miss Mapp had always felt herself equal to any social dilemma that might befall her, but even her resolute personality was momentarily nonplussed by the irrefutable fact that she, an unmarried woman of unimpeachable virtue, could be seen standing in broad daylight in the streets of Tilling talking to an unmarried man dressed impeccably in collar and tie above the waist, but below it simply in a pair of long woollen underpants of indeterminate hue. She quelled the instinctive shriek that rose unbidden in her maidenly throat, and decided that by far the kindest thing would be simply to ignore these circumstances.

'Good morning, Major,' she cooed, her eyes fixed determinedly on his face. 'I felt I should just see if everything was all right, as I thought I heard you cry out a little earlier. I wondered if perhaps you had cut yourself shaving?'

The Major's realisation that he was not wearing any trousers had come a second or two after Miss Mapp's, and roused in him a perturbation that was second only to her own. What on earth could he do? To slam the door in her face was an option, but could be quickly dismissed on the grounds of how rude it would look. To cower behind it with his head poking around the edge was surely unmanly. His eyes met her own fixed and somewhat desperate gaze and he decided in an instant to take his lead from her and pretend that nothing was amiss.

'Miss Elizabeth,' he said, and then he said 'Ah!' to give himself time to think. He said 'Ah!' a lot and found that provided he said it in various different tones of voice it answered pretty well for many situations. For example, if someone said something you did not understand, but which sounded rather clever, then saying 'Ah!' in the right way could convey the message 'Yes, I understand and agree with everything you're saying, although perhaps there are a few subtle nuances you may not fully have considered', which was infinitely preferable to standing there with a blank expression on your face. This tactic was frequently of great assistance during conversations with Mr Wyse, who was apt to mention someone with an Italian-sounding name and then bow significantly. If you said, 'By Jove, yes, that man could paint,' he usually turned out to be an opera singer and Mr Wyse would courteously try to mask his contempt for your intellectual failings, and almost succeed; could make a man feel jolly small, that.

He realised that he had used up most of the pause which an 'Ah!' could properly be said to command, and toyed with saying it again. This could be dangerous, as to say 'Ah!' once and significantly could be seen as the sign of a deeply thoughtful man who is pondering some complex abstract concept, whereas to say it twice could be seen as the sign of a deeply thoughtless man who has just realised that he is standing at his open front door with no trousers on. With difficulty, he continued the surreal conversation.

'No, no, quite well, thank you, dear lady,' he assured her. 'Perhaps it was a gull you heard? They are particularly noisy at this time of year, I find. Something to do with nesting, perhaps?'

'Ah yes, that must have been it. A gull, of course.'

Usually Miss Mapp would not have let her victim off so lightly, and would have remained on the doorstep, twisting the knife for as long as possible with tender enquiries after the Major's servant problem and state of health, but on this occasion she was understandably anxious to bring the interview to a close as quickly as possible. However, just as she started to bid the Major a smiling farewell, disaster struck. First the fishmonger's boy rode past on his bicycle and made a most inappropriate remark. This Miss Mapp could at least pretend not to hear, but she had no such option with the second cruel shaft which fate now fired in her direction. Immediately behind the first cyclist rode another, and who should it turn out to be but Quaint Irene, who rang her bell vigorously and hooted 'What-ho, Benjy! Bit eager today, aren't you?' as she disappeared round the corner.

Miss Mapp and Major Benjy looked at each other for a moment in horrified silence, and then with a muttered parting they went their separate ways, she to stomp in silent fury to Twistevant's, and he to sink in a pale and trembling heap on to a chair in his hallway. Major Flint had encountered various tricky situations during his army career, although not nearly as many as appeared with monotonous regularity in his recollections of military life, but nothing could compare to the hopeless, aching dread which he now felt at the prospect of having to open his front door (after having attired himself correctly, of course) and face his friends and neighbours. At times of extreme distress or uncertainty, particularly if coupled with mild inebriation, he was apt to draw himself to attention and salute, but even the thought of this did little to lift his depression on this occasion.

His morning had started badly. He was in possession of neither servant nor breakfast. He owed money to his wine merchant and, more dashingly yet more dangerously, to a bookmaker in Hastings. He had thought things could hardly get worse, and yet, clad in a pair of somewhat dingy combinations, he had just opened the door to the most redoubtable defender of Tilling society's respectability. He buried his head in his hands as he realised that he must shortly leave his house and face that very Tilling society who would by now, since news travelled fast among the basket-carrying classes, doubtless be in full possession of the facts.

In consequence it was some time before he put in an appearance on the streets of Tilling, shopping basket in hand as he walked stiffly in search of provisions. Mercifully Irene Coles was nowhere to be seen. Diva Plaistow was, however, walking towards him on the same side of the road and short of crossing the road to avoid her, which was plainly unthinkable, some effort at conversation was going to have to be made.

'Mrs Plaistow, good morning.' He raised his hat. For once, 'Any news?' did not seem an appropriate greeting. There was always the chance, he assured himself hopefully, that the 'news' of which he was himself the subject may not yet have leaked out. He could see instantly that such hopes were in vain. Diva Plaistow, who usually issued forth volubly yet telegraphically, was evidently in difficulties. Her larynx was going up and down with little gulping noises, but no recognisable words were emerging.

'Quite well, I trust?' enquired the Major.

'Yes, thank you,' uttered Diva at last, and then instantly decided to take refuge in flight. 'Would love to … can't stay … things to do,' she trailed behind her as she headed back in the direction from which she had come. The Major followed at a discreet distance. Damn! Here was Miss Mapp coming towards him and that was the very last thing he wanted at this precise moment, but there was nothing for it but to raise his hat again and say 'Miss Elizabeth' with as normal a countenance as he could manage.

Miss Mapp fixed a beatific smile upon him. She had decided to continue with her strategy of pretending that nothing at all out of the ordinary had happened. Unfortunately the Major himself now proceeded rather clumsily to forestall this.

'I feel I must apologise, dear lady, for the unfortunate incident just now. I hope you will understand that …' he searched for words, and decided upon 'a combination of circumstances'. Unfortunately the gear wheels in his rather stressed mind slipped and crashed, and what actually came out was 'a circumstance of combinations'. Miss Mapp blanched visibly. 'Combinations' was the one word which had been going round in her head for some time, and the one which she had hoped never to hear uttered again.

'Dear Major,' she said quickly, for who knew what he might say next, 'old friends as we are, perhaps we could forget the incident entirely. You will render me the greatest service imaginable if you would neither think of it nor refer to it ever again.'

Relief flooded into his face. 'Absolutely! Quite!' he said, and then another 'Quite!' for good measure.

Miss Mapp pinched the bridge of her nose and sighed deeply. Nobody could be resident in Tilling for very long without coming to recognise this as one of her 'Magnanimously though I am behaving, I am nonetheless deeply distressed and may indeed never recover' moments, and the Major had lived in Tilling longer than most.

'Decent of you, Miss Elizabeth,' he hissed fervently, 'damned decent, if I may say so. More than I deserve, of course.'

Miss Mapp released the bridge of her nose from her pained grip and smiled beatifically once more. Benjy took this as indicating that her moment of intense suffering had passed.

'And now, dear Major,' she continued briskly, showing that she was determinedly putting the whole sordid episode behind her, 'do tell me what you are doing to replace that wretched woman Sarah.'

'Ah!' This time it was a deeply heartfelt 'Ah', the meaning of which required no conscious modulation of tone. In it Miss Mapp read a whole story of untold suffering, of unprovided bacon and egg, unironed shirts and unpolished shoes. Perhaps this might be the time to renew her efforts to persuade the Major to abandon his fine manly reserve and surrender himself to the feelings of passion and irresistible attraction that he must perforce feel whenever he was in her presence; but the time was not yet. The more abject his position, the more ready he would be to surmise that perhaps her demeanour of girlish virtue may, reluctantly of course, be cast aside.

She cocked her head on one side in that curious birdlike way that all her acquaintances remarked upon ('Mapp's bird-of-prey look' was Irene's unflattering description) and gazed dreamily at the Major. No sooner had she done so than she rather wished she hadn't, for she found that with her head cocked to one side the sun was directly in her eyes and her dreamy gaze instantly became a watery squint which she was sure could not be at all becoming. She shifted her weight to the other foot so that she swayed into the Major's substantial shadow.

'Have you thought of widening the scope of your search?' she enquired.

The Major looked to be at something of a loss. 'How do you mean? Advertise for a valet instead? Or a butler? Bit beyond me, I'm afraid.'

'No, no.' Miss Mapp adopted the pitying look she always employed when dealing with men, which conveyed for anyone who cared to look (or to enquire if they remained in the slightest doubt) her amused though fond contempt for those who had no grasp of practical domestic matters. 'If the *Tilling Gazette* doesn't answer the situation then why not try casting your net further afield? Why not take the train into Hastings and try the *East Sussex Advertiser*, or even into Brighton and the *Sussex Chronicle*?'

Normally the Major's first thought would have been of the ruinous expenditure in train fares and advertising fees involved in such an endeavour, but today his thoughts of empty breakfast tables vanquished his finer feelings.

'By Jove, you're right,' he exclaimed. 'Of course you are. Why bless you, Miss Elizabeth, you always have the advice a chap needs to get him out of any fix. Can't think why I didn't ask you before.'

In truth Miss Mapp was very glad he hadn't, since the idea had only just come to her, but she bestowed upon him a final smile and said, 'Oh, you men are so helpless,' as she tripped homewards in a manner which she sincerely hoped was girlish.

Major Benjy stood undecided in West Street, a conflict of wants tugging at his emotions. On the one hand lay a round of golf on a sunny morning, followed by a few whiskies in the clubhouse. On the other lay a tedious train journey with a nonetheless necessary purpose. Prospects of long-term breakfast and supper triumphed over short-term gratification, however, and he strode purposefully to the station to check the times of trains to Hastings and Brighton.

While the Major's military tread was tramping towards the railway, an interesting scene was being played out in the public bar of a nearby public house, where Irene Coles could be discerned with a large Amazon, Lucy by name, and a nondescript man in a shabby suit, whose fingers seemed stained in equal parts by nicotine and ink, just as, it must be admitted, were Irene's own, though hers exhibited a more multicoloured hue since they bore the remains of just about every individual part of her armoury of paints. Lucy was variously described as Irene's maid, helpmate, muse, companion or model, depending on who was doing the describing and what their mood was towards Irene at the time. In truth the precise basis upon which the two shared Taormina, Irene's cottage, was something upon which polite Tilling society preferred not to speculate openly, though Major Flint, Mr Wyse and, until recently, the late Captain Puffin had done so privately on many occasions in the saloon bar of the Trader's Arms. Whatever conclusions these nocturnal symposia had reached had evidently done nothing to diminish either lady in Major Flint's estimation, as Miss Mapp noted frequently to her bitter disappointment. For Irene he maintained a comradely intimacy and they were often to be seen laughing loudly and suddenly during an otherwise respectable tea party, digging each other in the ribs in what she considered to be a positively common manner. Where Lucy was concerned he was apt simply to stand and gaze at her in rapt admiration, exclaiming 'By Jove!' as her statuesque frame proceeded majestically the length of the High Street.

The nondescript man, who had already bought each of them one pint of bitter, was looking at a piece of paper which he held in his hand and chuckling repeatedly as he exclaimed 'Upon my soul!' and 'You've caught them exactly!' A casual onlooker might have deduced from what they caught (accidentally and unwillingly, of course) of the conversation that the piece of paper was an artistic work by Irene and, the gentleman being the erstwhile editor of the *Tilling Gazette*, that she was attempting to interest him in its publication, and on this occasion the surmises of the casual observer would have been absolutely correct.

The representative of the fourth estate regretted deeply that he was unable to make use of Miss Coles's sketch, though he personally found it of great interest, and of course most skilfully executed. After having bought Irene and Lucy another pint of bitter each, he managed to extricate himself from the temptations of an extended lunch hour in the pub and returned to his office, still suffering from occasional fits of spontaneous mirth, leaving Irene gazing ruefully at her sketch and observing bitterly that once again the true extent of her talent had gone cruelly unappreciated. Save at the annual Tilling art exhibition, Irene's work languished mostly unseen and unadmired in her cramped studio at Taormina, though she had converted those windows of the cottage which overlooked the street into an impromptu gallery by displaying works up against the panes, from which position they could receive their proper due from passing art enthusiasts and (who knows?) potential purchasers. Somewhat dejected, but consoled by some excellent beer courtesy of the *Gazette*'s expense account and the prospect of steak and kidney pudding for supper, they headed homewards.

Miss Mapp was meanwhile giving her gardener his orders with all her customary firmness but quite uncharacteristic lack of attention. For one thing, the thought of her recent predicament still lingered as an unpleasant distraction. For another, her parting shot at Major Benjy had set a train of thought in motion, a train of thought which might quite possibly leave the branch line of prudent parsimony and launch itself on the mainline of unexpected riches. Every summer Elizabeth Mapp granted a summer lease of dear Mallards to some entirely undeserving individual and went to live for two months in Wasters, Diva Plaistow's house, while Diva rented Taormina from Irene. Irene and Lucy in turn moved into a fisherman's shack out of town near the beach and cycled in every morning to do their shopping, getting browner and more salt-stained, and exuding an ever heavier odour of fish as the summer progressed, their temporary dwelling's ablutionary arrangements being virtually non-existent and its sanitary provisions best left to the imagination.

These arrangements had hardened over time into a permanent part of Tilling's micro-economy, and for each participant represented a welcome cash windfall to help tide them over until the following summer. Miss Mapp benefited in addition by being able to reap nature's bounty from two gardens rather than one (since she cannily let Mallards on terms which excluded garden produce, but rented Wasters on terms which included it), and was able to bottle or make into jam everything which she could not sell to Twistevant's. For some time, however, Miss Mapp's fertile mind had been at work on how she might increase the shamefully small recompense which she received for grudgingly allowing a total stranger the use of her wonderful house. The assurances of whichever of Mr Woolgar and Mr Pipstow was so unfortunate as to be in the office when she came calling that the sums she received represented in every way a fair market rent did little to satisfy her. Why should she not take some of her own advice and cast her net more widely by advertising in the newspapers, rather than relying on the dubious merits of a card in Woolgar and Pipstow's window? Perhaps she might even give the Major the wording of her own advertisement to take with him, thus very sensibly saving herself the totally unnecessary expense of a train ticket? She reached for pen and paper and began to write.

As Miss Mapp finished her writing and laid aside her pen, she thought she heard the roar of a savage animal in the distance and wondered nervously if the bull from the farm just outside town had again broken down its fence and made its way into Tilling, as it had done a few months ago. Fortunately no harm had been done on that occasion before the farmer recaptured it, if one overlooks something dreadfully unfortunate which it did all over Diva's doorstep. As she put on her hat to hurry out in search of Major Benjy, she heard the roar again and hesitated over whether to open the door and brave the street. As she did so, however, she realised that there was something very familiar about that roar, and so it was more in curiosity than in trepidation that she finally set foot outside.

Major Benjy was striding up the road, his face red with fury, and slapping his walking stick heavily and repeatedly against his leg. As they met she turned an enquiring gaze upon him, but found that he was virtually incoherent with rage.

'Miss Elizabeth!' he spluttered. 'Never have I seen such a vile outrage – never!' He took her by the arm (an act which would in happier times have provoked a riot of modest emotions, perhaps even leading to the necessity for an application of smelling salts) and propelled her down the road. As they came level with Taormina he

14

poked a violent stick at one of its windows. There, for all of Tilling to see, was the sketch in which Irene had tried to interest the editor earlier that day.

The drawing was brief but effective. A few pencil lines had caught both Major Benjy and Miss Mapp so accurately that there could be no doubt as to their identity. The Major was standing framed in his own doorway in collar, tie and combinations, while Miss Mapp was gazing at him with a look of astonishment on her face. Behind them was a brief squiggle, which was undeniably the delivery boy on his bike, and a speech balloon captured his immortal line, which Miss Mapp had been trying so hard to forget: 'Show us yours, love, and we can all have a good laugh!'

As if this gross indignity were not enough, Irene had obviously been sufficiently interested in the scene to essay one or two variations upon it, and next to the original sketch was another. This was again in monochrome, but with the addition of a large pink blob representing the Major's nose, while this time Miss Mapp was also unclothed below the waist, her modesty protected by a voluminous pair of bloomers which were in exactly the same hue of pink. Miss Mapp decided that the time had come to faint and she collapsed with a little sigh. She preserved her presence of mind sufficiently to collapse in the Major's direction, and he gallantly caught her as she fell.

Chapter 2

Never had Elizabeth Mapp slept less soundly than she did the night following Irene Coles's despicable act. She burned and bubbled with fury at such a base overturning of all standards of decent social conduct (not that Quaint Irene ever bothered herself with such things, she told herself as she tossed and turned in the wee small hours), of such a blatant insult to her own reputation as the acknowledged leader of Tilling society. Yet at the same time she burned and bubbled with deep mortification, for disgraceful and inflammatory as the sketch had been, it had (the first one at least) been an undeniably accurate depiction of something which had actually taken place and she would have to face her fellow Tillingites on the morrow in the full knowledge that Irene's sketch would not only have been earnestly studied by all who could find enough excuses to walk backwards and forwards in front of it while engaged on myriad errands, but also endlessly discussed in tones of delighted horror and feigned outrage.

While news of the original incident had already spread around town in a matter of minutes in the wake of Irene's bicycle, Miss Mapp felt she had weathered the initial embarrassment, and surely nobody could have failed to be impressed by her steadfast dignity in refusing even to acknowledge publicly that anything untoward had occurred. Naturally, respect and neighbourly concern for her dear friend Major Benjy would have been discerned behind her saintly forbearance. A few might even have guessed, though had they done so she would naturally have disabused them of the notion with just enough fierceness that they would not have believed her, that still deeper emotions stirred in her womanly breast and made her all the more protective of the dear Major's lapse.

Yet the sketch had changed everything. Where once still deeper emotions might have been hinted at with a fetching sigh and a faraway gaze, hateful Irene had portrayed her and the Major as the centre of a vulgar scene in plain public view, and subject to the most grossly impertinent abuse by a common fishmonger's boy. Now people would be excessively polite to her face, but would giggle to themselves and make silly, hurtful remarks as soon as she walked away.

She deeply regretted that she had ever exchanged so much as a single civil word to Irene. Certainly from now onwards the door of Mallards would be firmly barred to her, and she would do her best to see that those inhabitants of Tilling who claimed to be her friends would act in similar fashion. This prospect of total social exclusion for her tormentor calmed her a little, and by and by she dropped off to sleep, enjoying delightful dreams of Irene undergoing interrogation at the hands of the Spanish Inquisition, while Major Benjy stood by impassively, robed as a cardinal but inexplicably leaning on a golf club.

The Major, while similarly enraged, was not similarly sleepless, since he had lubricated his own deeper emotions with a number of whiskies and soda, necessitated by his having had to visit the King's Arms for a spot of supper. He had decided against the Trader's Arms as he knew Mr Wyse habitually dropped in there for a pre-prandial drink, and had no wish to endure any of his comments on the happenings of the day. Mr Wyse's conversation, like his manners, was of a particularly exquisite nature. However, the Major's mind tended not to work in a similarly exquisite manner and so he was permanently suspicious that Mr Wyse was actually making fun of him, but doing so diabolically in a manner which he was unlikely to understand. There can be few prospects as frightful as saying 'Oh, quite!' enthusiastically, when actually endorsing some subtle slight against oneself.

The Major's slumbers drew finally to a close as he dimly heard the church clock striking. He counted the chimes, went wrong and made it ten, but got out of bed nonetheless. As he did so he became aware of a pain in his head, not the usual sort of headache to which he had become accustomed in the morning, but more of a soreness in a particular place on the top of his head. He moved a hand in exploratory fashion through his thinning hair, and winced as it encountered a definite lump. As he sat on the edge of his bed in his pyjamas, holding his head, a dim recollection came to him. His rage and courage boosted by several whiskies, he had banged several times on the door of Taormina on his way home and attempted to remonstrate with Irene Coles. His efforts had not been crowned with success. On the contrary, the admirable Lucy had seized his walking stick, hit him hard on the top of the head with it, so hard indeed that he had said 'Oh!' in a surprised sort of way and sat down very quickly on the pavement, and shut the door firmly in his face. He moved his other hand in the direction of the base of his spine and squirmed uncomfortably as a new source of bruising came to light.

He shaved and dressed, being careful not to knock either back or head against anything in the process, and taking the precaution of having a glass of fizzing Alka-Seltzer readily to hand. Before he opened his front door he felt cautiously to see if his trousers were in place, and found that all was well. Walking outside, he looked at his watch and found that it was indeed some time after ten. He conjectured darkly whether the knock on his head might not have rendered him unconscious, and briefly considered heading for the police station to lay charges for assault. Further consideration conjured up the vision of having to give evidence in front of all of Tilling as to having been knocked to the ground by a single blow from a woman, and he decided magnanimously to treat the matter as closed.

He walked towards Mallards and rang the doorbell. Much to his surprise his knock was answered not by Withers but by Elizabeth Mapp herself, gazing rather short-sightedly round the edge of the door and clutching a somewhat ineffectual dressing gown to her ample bosom.

'Why, Major Benjy!' she exclaimed with obvious delight but no little embarrassment. 'This is somewhat awkward; as you can see, I am *en décolletage*.'

Major Benjy knew little of any other language than English, despite his fabled fluency in Hindustani, but he knew enough to recognise a malapropism when he heard one. Miss Mapp should clearly have said *en déshabillé*, but her error was so endearing, not to mention attractively accurate, that he chose to ignore it.

'Dear lady,' he said gallantly, gazing fixedly at the territory some inches below her chin, 'we are, I trust, old friends …' At this stage the vista became altogether too distracting and he completely lost his train of thought. He became conscious that he was bending forward with what might have seemed to an ignorant observer a somewhat lascivious smile on his face. With an effort, he gathered his wits and managed an 'Eh, what?' which he trusted would suffice both to finish the sentence and to convey his intentions. As so often with Major Benjy, however, it succeeded in convincingly executing neither purpose.

'Dear friend,' Miss Mapp said in some confusion, 'as you see, I am in no state to ask you in, much though I would like to. I fear that I suffered terribly from insomnia last night and have only just arisen. Irene's sketch, you know – so hard to sleep. And just to make matters worse, some hooligans started shouting and banging on front doors just as I was dropping off. You will have heard them, of course? Obviously some passing drunks from out of town.'

'Ah!' said Major Benjy. 'Yes, quite.' He realised this would not be a profitable line of conversation to pursue.

'Was there something? Something in particular, I mean?' asked Miss Mapp.

'Yes,' said the Major determinedly, still regarding her chest in what he hoped would be considered a neighbourly and avuncular fashion, 'yes, there was. I mean, there is.'

'What is it?' enquired Miss Mapp.

'What?'

'What is it?' she repeated.

'No, I mean what is what?'

'What is it that you wish to speak to me about?' Miss Mapp spoke slowly and deliberately as though talking to someone who is very old, very deaf, or both. Major Benjy noticed this and took some umbrage at it. It was a bit off, he thought, if someone of his own sort of age should think that he, Major Benjamin Flint, late of His Majesty's Indian Army, was going gaga. Yet, he was forced to admit …

'I can't remember,' he said.

'You can't remember?' Miss Mapp's tone was one of genuine astonishment, yet he felt her mood teetering on the edge of the dangerous calm which she reserved for those to whom she wished to make it clear that she was humouring their simple ramblings much as she would those of a senile relative. The Major had been on the receiving end of this before, and had no wish to be so again. He decided to deploy the legendary Flint charm, and smiled in that manly yet endearing style that he knew was all his own.

'Dear Miss Elizabeth,' he said solemnly, 'I must confess that the sight of so striking an example of English womanhood standing before me has driven all other considerations from my mind.'

Fortunately for the Major, Miss Mapp's fabled modesty was of such a refined nature that it not only admitted of compliments, but feasted eagerly upon them. Major Benjy's honest, open admiration, so simply expressed, filled her sails and she giggled shyly, her cargo shifting dangerously as she did so, discomfiting her military beau still further.

'Dear Major Benjy,' she said in the quiet and intimate tone of voice which she used to practise when alone in her garden room in the hope that exactly this sort of situation would arise, 'you must remember that I am sadly inexperienced in the ways of the world, and take care not to turn a poor girl's head.'

The Major breathed a sigh of relief.

'Then let us say no more for the present, dear lady,' he murmured, raising his hat. 'Perhaps we shall meet later in the day? *Au reservoir* for now.'

'*Au reservoir*' was a totally original form of address that had been invented by Miss Mapp shortly after she came across it in daily use in Riseholme while on a visit there, and she had graciously consented to her creation being adopted as a feature of Tilling's social intercourse.

The Major turned away, his eyes fixed on the paving stones ahead, but seeing only a multiplicity of soft, fleshy bosoms. So intent was he on Miss Mapp's hitherto unexpected charms that he found himself in the thick of Tilling society almost before he was aware of it. Mr Bartlett, the Padre, affected a broad Scottish accent for reasons none could quite understand, since he hailed from nowhere further north than Birmingham, but this was felt to be a harmless nod towards eccentricity and therefore acceptable in any social circles, and consequently went unremarked upon. He bade the Major good day and observed that he was 'a wee thing late this morning'. His wife, Evie, told the Major in a voice so high-pitched as to be almost inaudible to the human ear that she had just chanced upon Diva coming out of Hopkins the fishmonger, but broke off in mid-sentence as she realised that this was treading dangerously close to territory on which she had been instructed not to stray.

Next he happened upon Mr and Mrs Wyse undertaking a rare ambulatory mission without the benefit of their Rolls Royce, and they too appeared studiously to be avoiding all mention of anything that might by even the merest association conjure up visions of trousers, bicycles or even fishmongers.

By the time Miss Mapp had completed her toilette and joined the strolling throng it had become clear that far from the overt solicitude and covert derision which she had anticipated and feared, the sympathies of Tilling on this occasion lay fairly and squarely with Miss Mapp and Major Benjy. It was universally agreed, once Diva had broached the subject with what Elizabeth could only describe (old friends though they were) as her characteristic clumsiness, that Irene really had Gone Too Far this time, and that Something Must Be Done.

Mr Wyse, having winced with the utmost delicacy when Diva blurted out 'Very wrong of Irene, I thought', bowed gravely and suggested that for once perhaps Miss Coles's artistic tendencies had triumphed over her sense of social decorum. As so often after Mr Wyse had spoken, the assembled company was left with the impression that his pronouncement had been so profound that further detailed discussion on the subject would be not only unnecessary but slightly disrespectful, and so they sighed deeply and nodded. Miss Mapp was alone in feeling the injustice of this, as she had been planning to give Irene a public roasting for quite a while longer, but in the face of such resolute Christian forbearance she was at pains to show that she was the most Christian of the lot, though in truth her real feelings about Irene Coles had much more of the Old Testament about them than the New.

She was also exceedingly puzzled. These vicious feuds flaring up and dying away in turn were the lifeblood of Tilling conversation, and they were usually carefully nurtured in an effort to make them last as long as possible. There was nothing more calculated to seize the interest of one's interlocutor in response to the traditional query 'Any news?' than the information that one Tilling resident was not talking to another, nor more satisfying than the sight of news-gathering activities being abruptly cut short as one or other protagonist walked past bearing an expression of martyred innocence. Why, then, should everyone be apparently so keen to bring this one to an end so quickly, especially as they had all instantly and quite understandably sided with Miss Mapp as the innocent party? Perhaps the spiritually uplifting presence of the Padre had some part to play, but she could not help wondering if there was something that she was missing. Healthy suspicion was one of the less unattractive features of her character, and her antennae were twitching.

Mr Wyse, clad today in plum-coloured velvet, was pursuing his theme of the need for calm forbearance.

'There are times,' he said, and then paused and wrinkled his nose carefully as if the sentiments he was about to express were of such exquisite delicacy that their very bouquet should be savoured like a fine wine. 'There are times when one is faced with inappropriate conduct on the part of another and should simply rise above it. In this way one's moral superiority is clearly established in the eyes of all right-thinking people, and the perpetrator can then simply be left to consider the error of their ways in the fullness of time.'

A murmur of approval ran around the group. The Major tugged the peak of his cap very gravely indeed, while the Padre beamed with approval and mentioned turning the other cheek. This was all very well, and Miss Mapp could happily have listened to many more remarks about her moral superiority, though her superiority in every way to that Coles creature was so self-evident as to need little elucidation even by so fluent an orator as Mr Wyse. Yet she felt undeniably peeved that he should have so cut the ground from under her feet that she could not indulge in the tirade against Quaint Irene that she had rehearsed in her mind before setting out from Mallards, basket in hand. She contented herself with saying 'Hmm' in what she hoped was a non-committal yet Christian manner, and if the others thought that she had actually pursed up her mouth in a very sour-looking way indeed, they had the good manners not to mention it.

'Well, I must awa' to the kirk,' said the Padre, and as the group broke up in a positive overflow of Christian good fellowship Miss Mapp realised to her chagrin that her moment had passed, and that to seek to raise the matter again would now be seen as a mean failure of character on her part after Mr Wyse's sage words, rather than as the natural outpourings of an innocent soul tortured beyond endurance. It really was too bad. She gripped the handle of her basket very tightly indeed as she stomped off to do her shopping. Her day was now quite ruined, and even the sight of the fishmonger leading that dreadful boy out of his shop by the ear in obvious pain and distress to apologise for his uncouth conduct the day before did little to mollify her.

Normally the ability to take infinite solace in the misfortunes of others could sustain her through any brief period of melancholy, but on this occasion even the very gratifying screams which the boy emitted as Mr Hopkins handled his ear none too gently offered little comfort. Something was 'up', she was sure of it, and whatever it was, everybody else was privy to it while she was not. There could be little more calculated to awaken an unsettled feeling in the centre of Tilling society than to suspect that it might revolve in circles which were not entirely concentric.

It was when she returned to Mallards that events began to unfold in a way which entirely confirmed her suspicions. Two envelopes lay waiting for her on the hall table. One, most surprisingly, was a brief note of apology from Irene for having 'overstepped the mark' and enclosing a pencil sketch of Miss Mapp's famous garden room window which, most unusually for Irene, was really rather good. The second was an invitation from the Wyses to tea and bridge that very day. Suddenly everything fell into place.

Bridge meant tables of four, and with Isabel Poppit, Susan Wyse's daughter and thus Mr Wyse's step-daughter, away in Italy that meant only seven people without Irene. She ran through the names in her head to be sure. Yes, the Wyses and the Bartletts made four, and she, Benjy and Diva made seven. So without Irene there could be no bridge, and clearly Irene could not have been asked if her appalling conduct had gone unappeased and unforgiven. In that moment Miss Mapp looked into the heart of Tilling and saw the blackness of its soul. Her so-called friends had been more concerned about saving their rubber of bridge than with supporting her at a time of emotional trauma. Never had she felt more betrayed.

It was fortunate indeed for her own peace of mind that Miss Mapp was incapable of being an honest judge of her own character. Had she been able to look into the innermost reaches of her own being, she would have recognised that she would just as readily have sacrificed any friend or compromised any principle for bridge, as would even the revered Mr Wyse or the undeniably Christian Reverend Bartlett, for bridge was to Tilling what a particularly juicy leaf was to a caterpillar. While the good citizens of Tilling might go to church regularly on a Sunday to pay their dues to the Almighty, the real religion which they practised revolved around a green baize tablecloth and two packs of cards.

Never, ever had anybody in Tilling been heard to say anything as infantile as 'Well, it's only a game' after a rubber of bridge, and had anyone been so naïve as to do so they would have been met with reactions ranging from bemusement to incredulity. The bridge table was a battleground, not so much in the subtle tactics of the game, which, it must be admitted, were largely lost upon Tillingites with the notable exception of the Padre, but in the sudden vituperative disputes which could be played out with vigour and venom during the course of a hand or two, and which left a distinctly awkward atmosphere should the cut of the cards determine that the object of your recent animosity was destined to be your partner for the next rubber.

Bridge was a drug, and an addict will go to extreme lengths to ensure that the supply of their drug is not disrupted. For the Padre or Mr Wyse to have slipped in to Taormina for a chat with Irene, or even to soften her resistance with a few cocktails, would not have disturbed the consciences of these worthy gentlemen one jot. All that mattered was that there should be two full tables for bridge that afternoon. For the same reason, while Miss Mapp naturally gave a great deal of thought to sending a note saying that she was still prostrate from nervous exhaustion and therefore unable to attend, such thoughts did not carry the day. The prospect of seven people trying to play bridge was a delicious one, and serve them right too, but the prospect of playing bridge herself that afternoon was even more compelling.

So it was that Miss Mapp presented herself at the Wyses that afternoon, wearing a smile of such fixed and glassy brightness that it could surely only be taken as representing the painful mask of one making a very noble sacrifice indeed for the sake of one's friends. To her dismay, however, none of the shallow individuals she had once thought her friends seemed to appreciate the depths of her suffering in the least. Susan Wyse, far from cultivating the slightly sombre air which a combination of sympathy and gratitude clearly called for, was, on the contrary, positively ebullient. As ebullient, thought Miss Mapp viciously, as only a very rich person with a Rolls Royce, a number of fur coats and the regalia of a Member of the British Empire negligently but prominently displayed in the living room could afford to be.

Such wealth did have its compensations, though, she reflected, greedily observing the candied fruits and chocolate éclairs dotted around the room. Such reckless extravagance was only to be expected from Susan. Miss Mapp herself pursued a line of sensible parsimony and typically provided rather stale seed cake on such occasions.

They cut for partners and Miss Mapp found herself playing with Evie Bartlett against the Padre and Susan Wyse. Miss Mapp pursued a highly complicated bidding system, complicated mostly since it was known only to her and, if truth be told, frequently developed as she went along, or even after the hand altogether. She described herself as an instinctive player, but this afternoon it seemed her instincts had deserted her. First she overcalled, and though she had clearly not intended her bid to be taken seriously (she had only a poor four-card suit) Evie, who also had four, squeaked her way impetuously to game, whereupon the Padre, displaying a lack of compassion which sat ill with his calling, doubled and inflicted a fourteen-hundred point penalty on them. At a penny a hundred, Miss Mapp was one and twopence the poorer after the very first hand. Next she had a genuinely good hand and bid confidently to game. Unfortunately the game she bid was in no trumps and the game which she tried to make was in hearts.

'Surely it was perfectly obvious that I had made an honest mistake?' she demanded. 'Why didn't somebody tell me?'

'No' for us to intervene, ye ken, Mistress Mapp,' said the Padre smoothly, marking up another hundred and fifty points to himself and his partner instead of the anticipated game to Miss Mapp.

'Well, I really do think you might have said something, anyway, partner,' she continued hotly to Evie Bartlett. Evie looked horrified and embarrassed in quick succession, and Susan had to intervene by reminding Miss Mapp that dummy was not allowed to say anything except to correct a revoke.

The use of the word 'revoke' was perhaps unfortunate since this is exactly what happened two hands later. The Padre, having already gained one game with a daring double finesse which Miss Mapp regarded as most un-British, now found himself struggling to make a four-spade contract into which his partner had put him rather over-enthusiastically. On the third round of spades Miss Mapp threw a club, at which the Padre gave a puzzled glance, but continued. Almost at once she realised what she had done, but alas it was too late to rectify the situation. In desperation she succeeded in sliding the offending card, a remaining spade, under the tablecloth, and dropping it on the floor at her feet.

'Hi,' she said suddenly when the Padre had only three cards left in his hand, 'how many cards do you have?'

It transpired of course that she had only two, while everyone else had three. Clearly, she declared, the initial deal had been badly conducted and the hand must be cancelled. The Padre, who had already worked out that he was about to go two off, was secretly relieved and was in the act of saying 'Och, weel' and throwing his cards on to the table, when hateful Irene Coles intervened.

'Hang on, Mapp,' she hooted, 'what's that on the floor?' So saying, she swooped on the two of spades and flourished it aloft.

Suspicion burned in every face but Miss Mapp's. The Padre was moved to venture that he had wondered what had happened to the thirteenth spade, when Miss Mapp discarded a club.

'Clearly I must have dropped it when I first picked my cards up,' said Miss Mapp briskly. 'So silly of me, I'm sure. Shall we redeal?'

The features of Mr Bartlett had contorted themselves into a most un-Christian expression. Doubt was struggling with compassion, and winning by a short head. At this stage the oracle, in the shape of Mr Wyse, gave voice.

Mr Wyse actually knew little more about the laws of bridge than any other Tillingite, although in the land of the blind the one-eyed man is king. Such was the gravity with which he expressed his opinions on these occasions, however, that they could clearly not be contradicted and everyone would say 'Ah, of course' very knowingly and try to look as if they had been perfectly aware of the fact and had indeed just been about to express it themselves.

'I think you'll find,' he opined sagely, 'that innocent though Miss Mapp's lapse clearly was, she is deemed to have had all the cards she was dealt in her hand throughout the game, and thus there was indeed a revoke, which has been established.'

'Aye,' said the Padre grimly, 'and as you won a subsequent trick, that's a two-trick penalty to us. Game and rubber, I think.'

Miss Mapp struggled to contain her mounting rage and forced herself to say sweetly, 'Why, of course, Mr Wyse, that's it exactly. Poor me to be punished so severely for such an innocent little slip.'

Normally Miss Mapp would have raged at great length about the unfairness of being penalised two tricks for a total accident that could have happened to anyone. Too late she realised that the others knew this well, and that her departure from character marked the

28

true nature of her 'accident' all too clearly. She fulminated inwardly against the injustice of the situation as she fumbled in her purse for a florin for the Padre. Then she realised that her partner had been Evie Bartlett and she quickly snatched it back and substituted a shilling.

'There, Susan,' she said, 'if Evie and I each give you a shilling, that makes it quits I think.'

Susan looked puzzled and Miss Mapp was forced to explain further. 'Evie and I each owe you and the Padre two shillings. So since he would presumably give his two shillings straight back to Evie to settle her own debt, it's easiest if we just give you a shilling each, so arriving at the same net result.'

She concluded her explanation, very pleased with herself for having summoned up 'arriving at the same net result' as a phrase, but the Padre was ahead of her. He may not have possessed any genuine Scots blood, but a long period of imitating the language had clearly had the effect of inculcating some basic Scottish characteristics, including unwillingness to see even the prospect of a shilling needlessly disappearing.

'Hold your horses a wee moment, Mistress Mapp,' he cut in swiftly. 'I think it's far better if I simply forgive the debt due from the wifie, and leave you to pay Mistress Wyse. Less complicated, ye ken.'

Susan Wyse had been looking increasingly confused as this tale of high finance unfolded, and she seized gratefully on the Padre's suggestion. 'I think that would be best, Elizabeth,' she said. 'Much simpler, I think.'

'Whatever you like, of course,' Miss Mapp replied, hoping by her tone of voice to make it clear that what she really meant was that if Susan was too stupid to understand her reasoning then there really was very little point in continuing the conversation. Unfortunately, her tone of voice and thunderous expression as the florin re-emerged from her purse made her true feelings all too plain.

The next cut of the cards left Miss Mapp and the Padre where they were, but brought them Mr Wyse and Quaint Irene respectively as partners. Miss Mapp assumed an air of pained but passive martyrdom, while Irene, presumably following delicate exhortations from Mr Wyse, was unctuously and uncharacteristically polite.

Part score succeeded part score but after a while each pair had scraped together enough points for a game, and so the match was all square. Quaint Irene's bidding was as colourful and unconventional as her painting, and so proceedings had not been without excitement despite the low scores, as the potential for a monumental misunderstanding with the Reverend Kenneth Bartlett, whose precise bidding was a subject for marvel and wonder the length and breadth of East Sussex, was ever present. Finally, it arrived.

Irene looked at the six small spades in her hand and confidently opened one spade. The Padre, who had a genuinely good hand, responded two hearts. Irene, trying to show that she really had a rather weak hand which it might perhaps have been better not to open at all, jumped to three spades, since she knew that three spades was a weak opening. The Padre, knowing that to jump in her suit Irene must have at least fifteen points, did some rapid mental arithmetic and bid six spades. Miss Mapp, holding the ace of diamonds, the ace of clubs and the king of spades guarded by two little ones, promptly (and rather viciously) doubled.

Miss Mapp pulled the ace of diamonds out of her hand and placed it complacently on the table. As she bestowed on Irene a snarl of incipient triumph, she became suddenly aware of two things. The first was that instead of the ace of diamonds she had actually pulled out a low heart. The second, which was rapidly borne in upon her by the startled expressions of the other three players, was that it was not her right to lead, but her partner's.

'So sorry – silly of me. It's Mr Wyse's lead, of course,' she ventured brightly, reaching out to retrieve the offending card.

'Hold your horses a wee moment once again, Mistress Mapp,' the Padre said evenly, reaching a hand across the green baize with the air of a man about to part the Red Sea. 'I dinnae think you can do that.'

'What nonsense!' Miss Mapp replied robustly. 'Why, it was obviously just a mistake on my part.'

'I fear the Padre is correct, partner,' Mr Wyse said reluctantly. 'I believe Miss Coles has various rights in a situation like this.'

'Oh, well, if she has rights then of course I must defer,' she responded with dark sarcasm.

The sarcasm, alas, went unheeded as Mr Wyse was by now quietly briefing Quaint Irene on what her options were. As soon as she learned that one of them was to accept the lead and ask her partner to play the hand with her own hand being tabled as the dummy she accepted with alacrity. After all, the Padre was by far the best player in the room. Affecting an air of unconcern, she tabled her dummy to reveal that far from fifteen points she had only six, the ace and queen of spades. Miss Mapp, realising that there was the potential here for a really significant penalty, felt her heart swell within her ample bosom.

It had to be admitted that the Padre's 'Thank you, partner' was somewhat clipped and perfunctory; he felt, with some justification, that his Christian nature was being sorely tested today. He studied the dummy intently, and as he did so the beginnings of a plan began to take shape in his mind.

Irene's hand contained six spades, two hearts, a solitary diamond and four clubs. The Padre won the first trick with the ace of hearts and then played a spade towards dummy. Miss Mapp ducked and dummy's queen was the winner. He then returned to his hand with Irene's second heart. At this stage Mr Wyse, who now held a singleton jack of spades, was a worried man. The Padre led the ten of spades from his hand towards dummy and to Mr Wyse's horror Miss Mapp, reciting 'Cover an honour with an honour' as she did so, played the king. Alas, dummy's ace now captured both the defenders' honours and the nine in the Padre's hand stood glittering and proud as the master trump. He played to it, Miss Mapp discarding her last trump, and then played out the queen of hearts, discarding dummy's only diamond.

Clearly declarer's problem now lay in clubs. He held four to the queen and jack, and so he was facing the prospect of two club losers. However, if Miss Mapp held four to the ace and Mr Wyse a singleton king, then it was just possible that she may be induced to play it, thus crashing her partner's king. Muttering an inward prayer, he played a low club. True to form, Miss Mapp's ace came down on the table with a cry of glee, cut short as Mr Wyse ruefully tabled the king.

Miss Mapp was troubled, but not yet disconsolate. She still held three clubs to the ten, and so felt certain of making her last club trick to take the slam down. With a feeling of gloating anticipation she considered her lead. Actually, even at this late stage all was not lost. In addition to her three clubs, the only other card now remaining in her hand was the ace of diamonds. All she had to do was to play it, forcing the Padre to trump on the table and then lead a club back towards his hand. Unfortunately the picture was not so clear to Miss Mapp, who, if truth be told, never bothered to count the cards anyway. She looked at the yawning void in dummy, where diamonds ought to be, and contemplated the horrid prospect of her ace of diamonds losing to a vulgar two of spades. No, it was not to be thought of. She led a low club, the Padre won it with a slightly higher one and tabled his cards, claiming his contract.

To bow from a seated position is not an easy accomplishment, but Mr Wyse executed it perfectly. 'Bravo!' he said in a rousing yet *mezzo forte* sort of way. 'Well played! Delightful!'

Miss Mapp's feelings were distinctly less charitable. She was sure that the Padre had used more of his advanced card-play techniques to win his contract, and regarded this as very unsporting. Still she managed to keep a damper on her discontent, and bit rather savagely into some candied fruit as she reflected on her misfortune. Even so her composure was sorely tested when Irene Coles came up to her, held out her hand with a smile of disgusting cheerfulness, and said, 'I make it one bob exactly, Mapp.'

Chapter 3

The following few days brought little to disturb the calm surface waters of Tilling's daily round, though both Major Benjy and Miss Mapp were waiting for their morning post with more than their usual anticipation. Indeed it was unusual for the post to hold any pleasurable anticipation for the Major at all, since he habitually received nothing other than bills present and reminders of bills past, and had in fact only the day before been in receipt of a most unpleasant communication from a bookmaker in Hastings to whom he owed five pounds. It was destined to be the Major's argosy that came home to the Rialto first, though. It would be wrong to say that he received a flood of applications, in fact the two envelopes that did duly plop on to his doormat could hardly be said even to constitute a trickle, but he was a pragmatic man and also an increasingly desperate one (lack of a proper breakfast was playing merry hell with his constitution) and so he summoned both applicants to Tilling for interview without delay by telegram, and hang the expense.

Such situations, we are told, frequently take the form of two closely matched candidates between whom it is monstrously difficult to decide. However, in this case the Major perceived an altogether more binary outcome. The first lady who presented herself was a thin woman with a very pinched and disagreeable expression who reminded him most unfortunately of the wife of his former adjutant, who had shown such temerity as to report him to the colonel for being drunk within the confines of the mess. Luckily the colonel had accepted at once that he had simply been overcome by a bout of malaria before being able to make it back to his billet, and that in such circumstances it had been entirely understandable for him to fall asleep face down on the billiards table, but memory of that rancorous woman cast a long shadow, and Major Benjy decided with a shudder that he simply could not have such a person living under his roof.

The second candidate, by contrast, was a delightful woman named Heather Gillespie, a war widow who had lost her husband on the Somme, at the mention of which a tear still sprang unbidden to her eye and the Major shifted uneasily in his chair and said 'There, there' and 'Dear, dear' with increasing embarrassment. She was a fine-looking woman in her mid-thirties with dark blonde hair and eyes of a quite piercing blue (Viking stock, perhaps, the Major mused).

A very inconvenient matter threatened to derail proceedings altogether, when it emerged that she was seeking a post as housekeeper, which was altogether much grander, and, he assumed, presumably more expensive than the more mundane position of 'servant' which he had in mind. Mrs Gillespie asked if the word 'housemaid' might define the Major's intentions, and he had to admit that it might.

At this Mrs Gillespie said 'Oh dear, oh dear' and started sobbing quietly to herself again. Between sobs she managed to explain that she had lately been engaged as housekeeper with a lady in St Leonard's and that, while nothing would give her more pleasure than to run the household of a military gentleman like the Major, she clearly could not be expected to take a step down in status. It would be similar, she pointed out, to the Major suddenly having to call himself 'Captain Flint'.

Major Benjy saw the force of this argument at once.

'By Jove, you're right. Of course you're right. I see it plainly now you put it like that.'

He could also see quite plainly that the knee which Heather Gillespie had inadvertently exposed as she crossed her legs was a remarkably fine one. She saw that he could see, and inadvertently exposed it a little more.

So, in little more than twenty minutes she had become the Major's new housekeeper, a prospect which seemed to fill her with infinite delight and which certainly filled the breakfast-deprived master of the house with the greatest relief. Pausing only to send for her luggage, she had sallied forth to buy provisions, and shortly after her return the smell of cooking filled the house.

On his return from the golf links, the Major was extremely pleasantly surprised to find freshly baked fruitcake awaiting him. Had he been more observant, he would also have noticed that living room and bedroom alike had been thoroughly cleaned, but he was a man of fixed and simple priorities, and fruitcake came a long way ahead of more mundane domestic considerations. Also awaiting him was an invitation to a dinner party at the Wyses. This was unexpected for two reasons. First, dinner parties were an unusual form of entertainment in Tilling, tea and bridge being the accepted norm. Second, it was generally understood that people entertained more or less in strict rotation, though Quaint Irene was usually held to be excused from this progression as people had become wary of visiting Taormina, which was strewn with tubes of paint, jars of turpentine and empty beer bottles, and whose solitary bedroom reminded those of delicate sensibility of the somewhat unconventional nature of the Coles ménage. The Wyses had of course only just held a tea and bridge party, and so it was most definitely not their turn.

Further perusal of the invitation explained all. Isabel had returned, bearing with her Mr Wyse's sister Amelia, more formally known as La Contessa di Faraglione, for a brief stay, and naturally the polite society of Tilling were bidden to dine with her. The Major said 'By Jove!' in an anticipatory sort of way, since the Wyses were known to employ a very good cook indeed, and to maintain a fine cellar. He helped himself to another piece of fruitcake, which seemed to have diminished in size rather rapidly now he came to think about it, and as Heather brought in more hot water for the pot he informed her, rather grandly as though this sort of thing happened all the time in Tilling, that he would be dining out with a visiting countess. She appeared properly impressed by this news, and bustled away to sponge and press his evening dress.

So it was that, splendidly attired in white tie and tails, the Major sat himself down carefully yet elegantly in his living room at seven o'clock while Heather poured him a large whisky and soda. Almost as she handed it to him there was a knock at the front door, which she went to answer. The Major had hardly had time to take a first ruminative pull at his drink when she returned with an envelope, which was addressed in what he instantly recognised as Miss Mapp's home counties copperplate. Tearing it open, the Major revealed it to be an impromptu invitation to take a chota peg with Miss Mapp before going on to the Wyses together. He gazed at the full glass already in his hand, tutted at the waste of it all, and promptly downed it in one. He was pleased to note that Heather stared at this feat with what might have been shock, but which could also have been admiration, so that he was almost tempted to repeat it, but instead took hat and stick in hand and strode the short distance to Mallards.

There was a short delay before Withers opened the door, as she was so recently returned from delivering Miss Mapp's note that she was still taking off her hat and putting on her apron. She looked understandably surprised to see him so soon, as Heather's response to her whispered explanation of what was contained in the note had been 'Oh dear, and I've only just poured the gentlemen his drink', but took his hat and stick without comment and led him into the living room, announcing: 'Major Flint, miss.'

'Dear Major Benjy,' said Miss Mapp, 'do mix yourself a chota peg the way you like it, and perhaps you might be so good as to pour me a small sherry?'

The Major happily obliged. There was some confusion as to exactly what a chota peg might be, although Mr Wyse had once offered, with a respectful bow to that revered scholar of Hindustani, Major Benjy, his understanding that 'chota' meant 'small'. If so, then 'chota peg' was certainly not an accurate description of the drink which the good Major was accustomed to enjoy, unless of course 'chota' referred to the amount of soda water dashed in grudgingly, almost as an afterthought. Indeed, the proper amount of whisky to put into a glass had been the only matter on which the Major and his good friend Captain Puffin had ever fallen out, apart of course from the unpardonable aspersions which his nautical neighbour had cast upon the character of Elizabeth Mapp, and which had embroiled all three of them in the mystery of the duel that never was. So far as the whisky dispute went, the whisky had been Captain Puffin's and the glass had been Major Benjy's, and had, in the Major's view, shown a considerable meanness of spirit in his friend which he had not previously suspected.

For the Major a chota peg meant a good fistful of whisky, and that was what he now poured himself. This was by way of being an unexpected pleasure, as Miss Mapp was not in the habit of issuing invitations to drinks. In fact, the Major reflected as he raised his glass to his benefactress, it had to be admitted that despite her many virtues Miss Mapp could quite honestly be said to be rather tight where alcohol was concerned, despite being reputed to keep an excellent cellar, second only to Mr Wyse's. If she was offering him the run of her Tantalus, then the chances were that she was expecting something in return.

'So tell me, Major,' Miss Mapp ventured, after sipping her sherry demurely, 'are you pleased with your new servant?'

'Well, early days, you know, Miss Elizabeth. After all, she only arrived this morning, what?'

'Of course, Major, but I meant to enquire as to what sort of person she is. Is she agreeable?'

'Oh, indeed she is. Yes, decidedly agreeable.'

The Major sensed that something lay behind this line of questioning, though he was puzzled as to what it might be. If he had known that Miss Mapp had observed Heather in the High Street on her shopping rounds, and been informed who she was by one of the shopkeepers, he would probably still have been none the wiser. To understand the situation at all, he would have needed to acquire a thorough appreciation of how the female mind worked, and in particular that startlingly individual example of it that resided within his interlocutor.

'She seems rather old to be taking up a housemaid's position,' continued Miss Mapp. 'I do hope that all the heavy work will not be too much for her.'

'Oh dear me, no, Miss Elizabeth, she's not old at all. And as for heavy work, I'm thinking of getting a girl in to do that once or twice a week. You see, Heather, Mrs Gillespie I suppose I should say, is going to be my housekeeper. But how kind of you to be concerned, Miss Elizabeth, and, if I may say so, how very like your good sweet nature.'

The Major was unsure what was afoot, but felt that throwing out random compliments could never be a bad idea, just in case. Miss Mapp was disarmed but temporarily, however, returning to the attack once more.

'A housekeeper? You surprise me, Major: you have never felt the need of one before. It sounds ruinously expensive, particularly if you plan to take in a maid as well, even if only once or twice a week.'

'Well, to tell you the truth, dear lady, I wasn't really looking for a housekeeper, but Mrs Gillespie seemed such a good sort that I felt I should stretch a point. After all, I was in desperate need of staff, if you remember.'

Miss Mapp was forced to concede this point, but promptly switched her attack to a different point on the Major's perimeter.

'And what about references?' she enquired.

'References?' The Major looked blank.

'Yes, references, Major. How on earth did you manage to take up her references so quickly. By telephone, I presume?'

The Major recognised when he was being thrown a lifeline, and he seized it gratefully.

'Ah, yes. Telephone, of course – just the thing, what?'

'And who were her references, if I may make so bold?' asked Miss Mapp sweetly. She knew that she was close to overstepping the mark, and was prepared to retreat swiftly yet gracefully if necessary. Yet she also knew that the Major was being less than truthful; for one thing, he did not possess a telephone.

'Oh, a Mrs Harrison in St Leonard's. Splendid lady – husband a bank manager. Said she had been very sorry to lose Heather – Mrs Gillespie, that is. Very sorry indeed.'

Miss Mapp did not look in the least satisfied by this explanation. As she drew breath once more, the Major desperately tried a pre-emptive three-level opening.

'And she is a war widow. I mean, after all, one has a sort of duty to one's former comrades, what?'

Miss Mapp recognised defeat when she saw it, and she saw it now in the shape of a demure form dressed entirely in black, standing forlornly before a war memorial.

'Well, of course, that is entirely different, I agree,' she said, and glanced at her mother's long-case clock, which stood surrounded by some of her collection of china pigs. 'Perhaps we should be making tracks, dear Major?'

Major Benjy breathed a sigh of relief, tossed back his second large tumbler of whisky in the space of a quarter of an hour and rose to open the door for Miss Mapp. Outside, he gave her a very gallant little half bow and offered her his arm. Taking it, she felt a decided tingle rush through her, and she forced herself to chat gaily of this and that as they strolled slowly towards Porpoise Street and the Wyses' abode, for all the world like a contented married couple.

It was of course their second visit to the Wyses in two days, and the only change appeared to be that Susan's MBE had been inadvertently placed in an even more prominent position, this time on the hall table where it could hardly fail to be seen as people left their hats and gloves. Unfortunately Susan did not seem to notice this until after the last guest had arrived, whereupon she gave a little scream of horror and snatched it up, exclaiming 'Oh, what will those servants do next?' as she did so.

Of course it was then only natural for all those in the room to take an avid interest in the regalia and beg Susan to show it to them all over again, despite her obvious reluctance. Reluctantly, she did so. It is, however, an ill wind that blows nobody any good, and, while everyone's attention was thus distracted, Major Benjy surreptitiously poured another few fingers of whisky into his glass, the level of which seemed to have dropped rather quickly in a quite unaccountable manner. As he insinuated himself back into the admiring circle, he was just in time to hear Miss Mapp say sweetly, 'Dear Susan, in all the many times I've admired your medal, I have never seen it looking so impressive. A pity you're not wearing your furs tonight; it would set them off so nicely.'

Perhaps fortunately, at this point the Contessa came downstairs and made her entrance. Miss Mapp briefly considered a curtsey but decided not to, partly because she remembered just in time that the Contessa had insisted on no formality on the occasion of an earlier visit, even to the extent of being addressed as 'Amelia', and partly because she was not entirely sure that, once having bobbed, she would be able to un-bob again in a suitably grave and non-wobbly fashion.

Amelia seemed to have been born with all the manly qualities which her brother lacked. She was a tall, dark woman, strongly built and with a loud voice. This latter accomplishment was a mixed blessing, as she knew little of tact, and did not share her brother's refinement of expression. It was, as Miss Mapp never tired of telling her fellow Tillingites when none of the Wyse clan were in earshot, so very strange that a count who owned his own island and presumably had the pick of Italian debutantes from whom to select a wife should have chosen so very unsuitable a creature as Amelia. Given the least encouragement she could wax lyrical on this theme for some time, even moving on to cast doubt on the very existence of the count, and thus on the validity of Amelia's title. 'Why,' she would cry, 'how do we know that Mr Wyse doesn't simply meet up with her every year in Bournemouth, or somewhere like that? I've always thought there was something very rum about Capri and all this faradiddly business.'

However, since the Wyse clan, or most of them, were very much within earshot at the precise moment, she contented herself with telling Amelia how very nice it was to see her in Tilling once again, and to enquire after the weather in Capri at this time of year.

'Bournemouth, you mean, surely, Elizabeth?' asked Diva brightly.

'No dear, how silly of you. Why, how deaf you're becoming as you get older! I clearly said Capri,' responded Miss Mapp, positively beaming with radiant goodwill. Unfortunately she was feeling such an abundance of goodwill towards Diva that she found her teeth starting to grind together, and she had to consciously loosen her jaw.

Isabel Poppit (or was it more proper to call her 'Wyse' now? Nobody was sure, and was careful to avoid any sort of social solecism by calling her either 'Isabel' or nothing at all) was quite late coming downstairs for some reason, and her mother had been casting increasingly irritated glances towards the dining room for some minutes when she did finally put in an appearance. Major Benjy, though, was not in the least unhappy about this as Susan Wyse pressed another glass of whisky upon him in the meantime.

The party moved into dinner and Major Benjy was glad to note that both food and wine were up to their usual high standard. He felt the warm glow of humanity engendered by five large whiskies spreading within him as he downed a few glasses of sherry with the soup, an excellent hock with the fish, and an equally superb claret with the roast lamb. In fact, by the time dessert had been served, the aforesaid glow had mellowed him to such an extent that he could only sit at the table, beam broadly at those around him and say

41

'Capital meal, quite capital!' At least, that is what he meant to say, but he seemed quite unaccountably to be having some difficulty with the word 'capital'. Susan Wyse gave him a worried glance, followed by a long meaningful one directed at her husband.

'Shall we, ladies?' she asked as she stood up. Major Benjy leapt to his feet to assist his neighbour, Diva, with her chair, bowing gallantly as he did so and gesturing expansively towards the drawing room. The gesture was perhaps a trifle too expansive, since he knocked over a candlestick, which set fire to a dried flower arrangement. With the instinctive 'Ha!' of a man of action, he seized a glass of water and threw it on to the miniature conflagration. This succeeded in extinguishing the flames, but left a soggy puddle in the middle of the tablecloth. By the time he had dabbed at this rather ineffectually with his napkin the ladies had left the room, and he joined his rather startled fellow males at Mr Wyse's end of the table.

Mr Wyse was torn between his concern for his dinner guest and the general well-being of his party on the one hand and his scrupulous duty as a host on the other. Consequently the port decanter stood at his elbow for quite some time while he affected to have forgotten all about it, but when the Major moved from ostentatiously picking up his empty glass and staring into it, to actually saying, 'I say, old man, do give the port a fair wind, there's a good chap,' there was little he could do except to say, 'Oh, I am so sorry,' and comply.

The Major had embarked upon the story of how he had saved the Maharajah of Peshawar from a man-eating tiger while armed only with a sword, but the narrative had become somewhat rambling and confused, as he kept breaking off to ask the table if they could imagine being a maharajah with two hundred nubile young wives and plentiful supplies of sesame oil, enquiries which left Mr Wyse looking impassive, the Padre genuinely bewildered and the Major gazing dreamily into space.

'And the tiger, Major?' asked Mr Wyse, in an effort to end this lengthy excursion on the branch lines of the Major's reminiscences.

This effort to switch the points was at once successful, as with a 'Ha, the tiger, eh?' the Major swept majestically back on to the main line and gathered speed towards the dénouement. He rose to his feet as the climax approached and demonstrated with a sweep of his arm the stroke from the Indian army swordplay manual with which he had severed the tiger's windpipe. This closely resembled a vigorous backhand volley from the baseline of a tennis court and made perfect contact with a wineglass, which hurtled across the room and shattered against the fireplace.

Mr Wyse rose magnificently to the occasion.

'What a wonderful story, Major, and what a marvellous demonstration of army swordplay. Why, a wineglass is a small price to pay for such entertainment!'

He stood up, bowed to a bemused Major Benjy and continued briskly: 'And now, I really do think we must join the ladies.'

The gentlemen dutifully trooped into the drawing room, where Susan was presiding over a fresh pot of coffee and Amelia was talking of Mussolini.

'You know an Irish woman tried to assassinate him a few years ago?' she demanded of nobody in particular, but in a voice whose volume suggested that she may require an answer from someone at the other end of the High Street. 'Of course, they said she was mad, poor woman ...'

The Major found his attention wandering. He could not help remembering that there had been what looked like a decent slug of whisky left in a bottle which he had just passed, obviously put down and forgotten about, on the hall table. Glass in hand, he slipped out of the room.

He was sure that Mr Wyse, perfect host that he was, would not begrudge a guest a small whisky. However, he realised that being seen helping himself to a drink uninvited could be open to misinterpretation, particularly by Miss Mapp (he shuddered inwardly at the thought of her fixing him with a disapproving stare and asking him what he was doing lurking furtively in the hall) and so, it being a fine night, he decided to open the French windows in the dining room and step into the garden.

He took a few paces on to the terrace, but it was dark and he quickly found that a moment arrived when his next step, instead of landing comfortably on a reassuring paving stone, dropped abruptly by about two feet and came unsteadily to rest on damp grass. He managed to keep his footing, but only at the expense of taking a few running steps in an effort to regain his balance. It was at this point that he encountered the Wyses' fish pond. With a bellow of surprise he measured his length, twisting as he did so, and found himself lying in about eighteen inches of water, half on his back and half on his side, having fallen most painfully on his elbow.

In the drawing room there was a moment's silence at the sound of a loud shout followed by a prodigious splash. Burglars! The thought flashed through the collective drawing-room mind. The Padre, who in his youth had been the middleweight boxing champion of the southern counties seminaries, snatched a poker from the fireplace and led the party out on to the terrace to investigate. Mr Wyse headed in the opposite direction, calling out to the Padre to wait a moment while he switched on his new electric lighting system in the garden.

Mr Wyse threw the switch and the Major found himself most unexpectedly bathed by floodlights, turning night into day in the space of a split second. Startled, his first attempt to extricate himself from the pond failed, and he fell rather messily back into the water. By the time he had picked himself up and tried peering into the lights to see what on earth was going on, Mr Wyse had arrived on the terrace. Major Benjy became aware that he was being stared at by quite a number of people. Partly to give himself time to think and partly because it was something which he habitually did when he could not think of anything else, he drew himself smartly to attention and saluted. Unfortunately he had forgotten that he was still holding the whisky bottle in his right hand.

As the Major hit himself on the head vigorously with the bottle, the dinner party company watched, mostly with alarm and concern, though with open hilarity on the part of Quaint Irene. The effect was rather like the immediate aftermath of the shooting of a rogue elephant. First the Major's face acquired a rather crumpled appearance, then he sagged at the knees and then fell, very slowly and as though with immense weariness, back into the fish pond.

Miss Mapp gave a scream which all afterwards agreed had struck exactly the right combination of shock and sympathy, while also hinting at barely repressed hysteria. The Major was removed from the pond by the Padre and Mr Wyse, still firmly gripping glass and bottle, both of which were now largely full of muddy water. Irene and Diva managed to prise them from the Major's shocked grip, while Susan Wyse went in search of her servants. Miss Mapp slumped on a garden bench giving a perfect impression of one having a fit of the vapours, while Evie Bartlett administered smelling salts.

The Wyses' chauffeur was summoned, travelling rugs were placed in the back of the Rolls Royce, and the Major was then installed on the back seat. This operation was not quite as straightforward as it might seem, as the Major was by this time attempting to brush off anyone who was holding him, saying repeatedly ''Sall right, old man, 'sall right.' Eventually, however, he was driven the few yards round the corner back to his own house, sitting bolt upright and holding on to the back of the front seat with a look of intense concentration on his face.

Perhaps unsurprisingly, the party broke up soon afterwards and the company sought their respective beds, shaking their heads sadly for the most part over the events of the evening, though eyeing the morrow with eager anticipation. There was universal agreement that never had Tilling witnessed such excitement, not even on the famous afternoon when Mr Wyse had been observed kissing Susan Poppit, as she then was, in the very same garden.

Morning found Mr Wyse wrestling not with Susan amid the flowerbeds, but with the *Times* crossword over a second helping of toast. His enterprises had been remarkably successful this morning; in fact there was only one clue remaining, but try as he might he could make no sense out of it at all. Susan, also a crossword enthusiast though one of lesser skill, had been enlisted but found wanting. 'African ill makes small William precede a king in foggier-sounding conditions.' What on earth could it mean?

As he considered calling for another pot of coffee to aid the cognitive process, a knock at the door heralded a note borne by Heather Gillespie and written, very shakily, by Major Benjy. It was brief but to the point, in classic military fashion. It asked Mr and Mrs Wyse to forgive his actions the previous evening, which he realised could be open to misinterpretation, but which had in fact been due to a sudden attack of recurrent bilharzia.

Miss Mapp had spotted Heather walking past the window of her garden room, envelope in hand, and had been in no doubt as to her destination. She hurried out in hot pursuit. Fortunately the Wyses' maid had just opened the window to air the room and it took little effort to pause outside it, gazing at her shopping list, finger on lips and with a thoughtful expression on her face, as though sure that she had forgotten something. Her efforts were not in vain.

Mr Wyse suddenly shouted 'Ah-hah!' and threw the Major's note on to the table in great agitation. Miss Mapp shook her head sorrowfully and went on her way. So she missed the sight of Mr Wyse picking up *The Times* and running into the next room to show it to Susan, though her acute hearing did catch him shouting, 'Come and look at this nonsense, Susan!'

Miss Mapp's purposeful progress towards the fruiter was arrested by an encounter with Diva Plaistow, whose 'Any news?' had a certain horrified awe about it. It was not, after all, every night that a Tilling resident, even the Major, hit himself over the head with a whisky bottle and fell in a fish pond.

'There certainly is,' replied Miss Mapp grimly. 'What do you think has happened? The Major has sent some ridiculous note to the Wyses attempting to explain his appalling conduct last night. Well, I suppose he thought he had to do something, but far better just to come clean in my view.'

'No!' exclaimed Diva in gratifying fashion. 'And what did the Wyses say?'

'They haven't responded, nor are they likely to of course. Mr Wyse threw the note across the room and shouted, positively *shouted* mind you, to Susan to come and look at this arrant nonsense, or something like that.'

'No!' said Diva again. 'Mr Wyse shouting? I can't believe it.' She gazed doubtfully, and a little short-sightedly, at Miss Mapp.

'Believe it!' retorted Miss Mapp hotly. 'I heard it with my own ears and saw it with my own eyes.'

Evie Bartlett had now joined the group and listened with fascination as Miss Mapp quickly brought her up to date as well. Enjoying her rightful station in life as the centre of attention, Miss Mapp felt it incumbent upon her to develop the narrative a little for the benefit of those who were not so quick on the uptake as she was.

'Mr Wyse used very strong language for him. In fact, as I was walking away I thought I heard him say something about not speaking to Major Flint again until he had apologised like a gentleman.'

'Crikey!' exclaimed Diva. 'That *is* serious.'

'Oh dear,' said Evie Bartlett despairingly, 'another rift is the last thing we need. Why, it was only a few days ago that Kenneth managed ...'

She suddenly realised that she was addressing one of the protagonists of Tilling's last rift, and broke off abruptly with a little squeak. Miss Mapp pretended not to notice and strode off with a cheery '*Au reservoir*'. However, she had only gone a few steps before she stopped abruptly and pinched the bridge of her nose very hard, clearly still deeply affected by the memory of the Quaint Irene affair.

'Are you all right, Elizabeth?' asked Diva reluctantly, for she recognised the 'deeply affected' stance and knew that failure to provide the required response would itself be seen as a mortal insult.

'Yes, quite all right, thank you,' replied Miss Mapp with a loud sniff, and walked on to complete her task of spreading the news of imminent internecine conflict, dabbing her eyes ostentatiously with a handkerchief as she did so.

Chapter 4

I t was at least eleven o'clock that morning before Major Benjy ventured gingerly from his house. The effects of bilharzia had obviously worn off just enough for him to attempt his usual morning constitutional, but the ravages it had effected upon his manly frame were plain for all to see. It was a pale and trembling shadow of his normal ebullient self that set forth that morning, shopping basket in hand.

As fate would have it Major Benjy, being late embarking on his round of shopping, was setting off while everyone else was already returning: the Wyses in the Royce, and everyone else on foot. The pregnant encounter for which everyone had been secretly longing after hearing Miss Mapp's dramatic summary of the situation was therefore not long delayed as the motor car forced the Major to move out of the centre of the road where, like any self-respecting Tillingite, he had naturally been walking, on to the pavement, so that the immense vehicle could squeeze past him.

Tilling society held its collective breath. Would the Wyses cut Major Benjy altogether, affecting not to see him, or would Mr Wyse correctly but coldly raise his hat the merest trifle as they passed? Majority opinion favoured the latter course, for Mr Wyse's manners were known to be perfect, but there was nonetheless a vociferous minority (Miss Mapp) who held that this time Mr Wyse had been pushed beyond endurance and may well so far forget himself as to fail to notice the Major: not just today, but for several weeks to come.

Tilling was accordingly entirely unprepared for what came next. The car glided to a halt, Mr Wyse shouting 'Stop, stop!' to the driver, and Mr Wyse jumped out and positively rushed towards the Major. Surely he was not going to descend to fisticuffs in the middle of the High Street? Or perhaps Tilling was finally going to witness the duel of which they all felt they had been unfairly deprived by the sudden rapprochement between the Major and Captain Puffin (if indeed this version of events could be believed at all).

Yet no! To the total astonishment of the several onlookers, all of whom had taken good care to continue walking so that they might not miss the slightest nuance of the looming confrontation, Mr Wyse managed at the same time to both raise his hat and shake the Major's hand, pumping it vigorously up and down.

'My dear Major,' he cried, 'this is an unexpected pleasure to see you out and about so soon. May I trust that you are making a steady recovery?'

The Major gurgled something incomprehensible, being largely occupied with the task of trying to speak without moving even the smallest part of his head, which was troubling him greatly.

'My dear sir,' Mr Wyse continued solicitously, 'is this sensible, to be walking abroad in your condition? Brave, yes. Manly, certainly. But, I venture to suggest, hardly sensible. Yours is a most serious illness, I believe.'

The Major managed to thank Mr Wyse for his concern, indicating that the condition 'came and went' and that he was just on his way to the chemist for some quinine.

'Talking of quinine, Major,' said Mr Wyse slyly, 'perhaps you would join me later for a gin and tonic at the Trader's Arms? I have something to celebrate, you see. Today is the first time in over five years that I have managed to finish the *Times* crossword, and it is entirely due to you. I am eternally in your debt, I find.'

Unusually, the thought of a gin and tonic actually made the Major feel extremely bilious, but he accepted with grace on condition that the enjoyable event might be postponed until the evening.

'Delighted, delighted,' beamed Mr Wyse, raising his hat to all and sundry, and reinserting his slightly corpulent frame into the back of the Rolls Royce. It departed with the gentle purr that high-quality automobiles emit on these occasions, leaving Miss Mapp in a somewhat exposed position as the leader of a lynch mob that was now apparently expected to transform itself suddenly into angels of mercy – stretcher bearers, perhaps.

Not even the brief relief afforded by the thirty seconds or so that it took the Major to raise his hat and continue rather painfully on his way could bring into her mind anything even vaguely credible as an explanation of so completely unexpected an outcome. She fixed a slightly vacant smile on her face, and proceeded to make the best fist of it that she could.

'Dear Mr Wyse,' she said dreamily, 'so charitable, so Christian. Why, what an example is there for us all. Such forgiveness!'

'Give it up, Elizabeth,' said Diva at once, most unhelpfully. 'You've got it all wrong as usual.'

'I hope, Diva dear, old friends as we are, that you are not doubting the evidence of my own eyes and ears?' asked Miss Mapp severely.

Irene snorted. 'Come off it, Mapp! The only thing you got wrong was not to spy on the Wyses through their window for a bit longer – then you might have got the full story.'

Really, Quaint Irene was most hateful on these occasions, and hate her Miss Mapp duly did. While she adopted an expression of noble suffering at such calumny, Irene stuck her pipe in her mouth and wandered off, snorting with laughter. For her part Diva simply said, 'Hmm, well …' in a generally disbelieving sort of way, and headed off. The Padre raised his hat absent-mindedly in parting without saying anything, and Miss Mapp found herself suddenly alone. This would not do at all. Fortunately the Major was not moving very quickly this morning and to catch him up was the work of but a few minutes, even though the exertion required caused her to go very red in the face.

'Dear Major Benjy,' she puffed, hoping that shortness of breath would not cause her to lapse into Diva-like telegraphese, 'so nice to see you out and about.'

The Major, unsure whether this was a signal of genuine solicitude or a prelude to a lecture on the evils of drink, but suspecting the latter, contented himself with saying 'Dear lady' and raising his cap while he waited to see whether Miss Mapp's sneaky approach to her jumping-off position would be followed by a full frontal assault with fixed bayonets. However, for once Miss Mapp seemed less than sure of her ground.

'I couldn't help overhearing,' she said, 'that Mr Wyse referred to you having a serious illness. Old friends that we are, I would have hoped that you might have confided in me.'

'Ah,' said the Major.

'After all,' she persisted, 'we are more or less neighbours, and if you were to be taken ill during the night I hope that I would be the first port of call should anyone wish to summon assistance.'

'Ah,' said the Major again. This time, however, Miss Mapp did not seem inclined to continue but simply stood there expectantly with her head slightly on one side. Clearly some response was required.

'Kind of you, Miss Elizabeth,' he said. 'Damned kind, in fact. The thing is, I had a twinge of the old bilharzia last night. Embarrassing, don't you know, because the awkward thing is that the symptoms can look pretty much like a chap who's had a few too many. Dare say there were some last night who thought that really was the case, what?'

Miss Mapp demurred courteously; in the circumstances any other response would have seemed churlish. She was uncomfortably aware that the Major seemed to have her at a disadvantage, not least because she had no idea what bilharzia was. This was not a sensation that she had experienced before, and she was becoming rapidly aware that it was one which she actively disliked.

'Is it usual to make such a rapid recovery?' she enquired. The Major knew a flank attack when he saw one and moved swiftly to repel it.

'Rapid recovery?' He gave a sincere groan. 'Dear lady, if you only knew. Thought I'd put a brave face on it, you see. Fact is, I'm feeling very dickey indeed. Very dickey indeed.'

Miss Mapp clucked sympathetically and insisted that the Major should go straight home. He promised to do so just as soon as he had bought himself some quinine at the chemist's. He raised his hat again and went rather stiffly on his way. Their paths diverged as Miss Mapp headed towards the public library. This was a regular weekly destination, but today's was an impromptu visit as no book nestled in her shopping bag, and upon entering she made her way with determined tread toward the unfamiliar surroundings of the reference section.

She noted with surprise that Diva must have preceded her, because there she was seated at a table, copying something out of a book. So preoccupied was she that Miss Mapp was able to sidle gently up behind her for long enough to see over her shoulder that it was a recipe for single-layer chocolate cake. She sidled away again equally imperceptibly, and went in search of a book on tropical diseases.

The Major headed as indicated into the chemist's, but it was not quinine but the largest available container of bicarbonate of soda that he loaded into his shopping basket and covered with the newspaper before heading homewards. Once there he sank heavily into an armchair and gave a truly piteous groan. Heather Gillespie hurried into the room with a glass of water, into which she mixed two large spoonfuls of the Major's newly purchased restorative. He duly swallowed this, but felt little different. While walking home he had experienced the unusual sensation of the paving stones heaving gently under his feet as if they were waves rather than a solid surface, and now he could have sworn that every time he looked at the walls of the living room they were coming a little closer. As for the clock, its loud ticking was becoming quite intolerable and its face was grinning at him with what could rightly be described as malevolence.

Heather Gillespie seemed to have had extensive experience of dealing with bilharzia patients, since she applied a cold compress to his forehead and suggested gently that he return to bed for forty winks.

'You dear, brave man,' she said. 'What courage it must have taken to go out to the shops as if nothing was wrong, just so your friends should not be unduly concerned about you.'

Major Flint was forced to admit that this was true. Heather removed the compress and patted his hand.

'But now, surely you don't need to pretend any longer?' she asked. 'A good sleep is what you need. Sleep as long as you can, and I'll bring you up a nice cup of tea when you wake.'

This seemed an eminently good idea and he dragged himself up the stairs and then dropped on to his bed fully clothed, with a sense of coming home after a particularly trying journey. His eyes were closed almost as soon as he hit the mattress.

While the Major slumbered deeply and morning turned into afternoon, the good ladies of Tilling were gathered at the vicarage under the aegis of Evie Bartlett, deep in discussion. The subject was not, as might have been expected, Mr Wyse's astonishing conduct of a few hours previously, but the annual Tilling Spring Show, to be held a few weeks hence. The Spring Show, the Summer Fete, the Art Exhibition and the Autumn Fair provided steady landmarks of the year's progress, a chance to show off new outfits and perhaps to invite the occasional visitor from the world beyond Tilling. Mix in jam-making, Harvest Festival, Christmas, spring cleaning and Easter, and the great marker stones of the year's progress (or its 'Eleanor crosses', as a Tillingite would surely suggest) stretched reassuringly ahead. Miss Mapp, as self-acknowledged leader of informed opinion, would frequently say, 'You know, I always think of the Spring Show and Harvest Festival as the two book-ends on the bookshelf of the summer,' and then gaze dreamily into the distance with a ferocious smile on her face.

Today, Evie Bartlett was on her home ground both physically and figuratively; there could be no dispute that it was the vicar's wee wifie who was the only proper person to act as *châtelaine* of this particular event, which was to be held in the church hall. This public acknowledgement of her leading position (no matter how temporary it might be in Miss Mapp's estimation) lent her an unusual air of self-confidence.

'Ladies,' she said, having replenished the plate of fruitcake between Diva Plaistow and Miss Mapp, which seemed somehow to have become emptied, 'we really must reach a decision on the domestic duel.'

This somewhat alarming expression referred to nothing more violent than an annual competition between the ladies of Tilling to demonstrate their prowess in some area of housekeeping or other womanly endeavour. Some years previously Mr Wyse, hosting the planning tea while the vicarage was being redecorated, had been begged to join the company, though his sex would normally have precluded his presence, and had thoughtfully but with his usual charming reticence suggested 'a sort of domestic duel', and like all Mr Wyse's suggestions this had been adopted enthusiastically, respectfully and unquestioningly.

Yet what should it be this year? The distressing business of last year's jam competition was still fresh in everybody's minds, though nobody was so tactless as to refer to it openly (Quaint Irene not being present), and knitting and needlework had been the weapons of choice in the two previous years.

Diva paused in the act of conveying another piece of fruitcake to her mouth and suddenly, with the air of one who has just experienced a divine revelation, suggested: 'I say! Why don't we make it a cake-making competition?'

This suggestion was met with universal acclaim, or at least almost universal, but Miss Mapp was not quite quick enough to get her objection in before the murmur of approval, and so she contented herself with saying, 'Hardly very original, Diva dear,' and then, as others glanced at her with what might very well have been the beginning of a frown, except of course that surely nobody could be so ill-mannered as to frown at Miss Mapp, 'but of course, if that is the mood of the meeting ...'

Suspicion is a healthy emotion, and just now Miss Mapp was beginning to feel healthier by the moment. Entries submitted for the domestic duel had to be the duellist's own work, and Miss Mapp was not in the habit of making cakes, leaving such things to Withers. Some of the other ladies, however, were once- or even twice-weekly bakers. Diva, in particular, was locally acclaimed as something of a Leonardo da Vinci in the *gateau* department, but then so was Evie Bartlett. Miss Mapp felt a definite but familiar tingle of the scalp, which denoted that there had been dirty work at the crossroads and that Diva and Evie had discussed this contentious subject in advance. The memory of Diva copying out the chocolate cake recipe in the library that very morning came flooding in upon her, and suspicion hardened into the cold fury of certainty. However, there was little she could do but to accept the situation with as good grace as she could muster.

'And who should judge it – Mr Wyse, do you think?' enquired Evie Bartlett. Yes, of course, agreed everyone, it should be Mr Wyse. It was always Mr Wyse. The party broke up with every appearance of smiling sisterhood.

Outside, however, finding herself alone with Diva, Miss Mapp lost no time before giving vent to her feelings.

'So clever of you, dear, to cook up that little scheme with Evie. If "cook" is not a sensitive word, that is. Hah!'

'I really can't think what you mean, Elizabeth,' replied Diva. 'Just like you, though, to spot plots and conspiracies where none exist. You should watch that.'

Miss Mapp was moved to righteous ire. 'Diva, dear, I sometimes wonder how you can bring yourself to go to church on Sunday. I am referring of course to the obvious skullduggery of choosing baking as this year's duel. The whole of Tilling knows that you and Evie regard yourselves as the denizens of cake-making – and I saw you copying out a recipe in the library only this morning.'

'I think you mean "doyennes", dear,' said Diva in pedagogic mode. 'Denizens are regular customers, I believe, rather like Major Benjy at the saloon bar. Perhaps you could help Mr Wyse with his crosswords – might improve your vocabulary.'

'Pray do not attempt to deflect attention from the real issue, Diva,' came Miss Mapp's icy rejoinder. 'You surely cannot deny that you and Evie Bartlett indulged in some very dirty work indeed to get your own way.'

'Firstly, Elizabeth, I recollect that everyone present, including incidentally yourself, was in agreement, and secondly I am very surprised that you should be raising the possibility of skullduggery after the affair of the jam last year.'

Miss Mapp gasped. This was definitely hitting below the belt, not least since the two of them had specifically agreed some time ago that the whole affair was Definitely Closed. 'I can't think what you mean,' she said.

'You know exactly what I mean,' said Diva emphatically. 'Passing marrow off as greengage like that – honestly!'

'It *was* greengage!' insisted Miss Mapp fiercely. 'I should know, I bottled it myself.'

'Greengage my eye,' asserted Diva. 'I know greengages when I taste them, Elizabeth, not that I ever have in your house – keep them for yourself, I suppose.'

Miss Mapp chose to ignore this slur on the bounteousness of her hospitality, though she stored the insult away to ruminate upon later.

'Diva dear,' she said, adopting the tone of an adult tried almost beyond endurance by a recalcitrant infant but giving them one last chance to avoid being sent to bed early without any tea, 'many of my jams contain a special ingredient. It is this that makes them so – well, special. It is largely for this reason that my preserves are the talk of East Sussex garden shows. You must expect a secret ingredient occasionally to impart a slightly different taste from what would otherwise be a well-known fruit flavour.'

'That was marrow,' maintained Diva stubbornly, 'and it was off. Poor Padre and Evie were ill for a week. Lost five pounds, Evie said. The only secret ingredient you could have put in that jam was castor oil, Elizabeth.'

It was rare for Diva to attain the last word in these exchanges, but on this occasion she succeeded in stalking off with a very satisfied expression on her face, leaving Miss Mapp spluttering and temporarily (and very unusually) speechless with rage.

The affair of the mystery jam had indeed been the talk of Tilling for some weeks the previous year, particularly since the Padre had at one stage been so ill as to be collected by ambulance in the middle of the night and taken off to the cottage hospital 'just as a precaution though', as Miss Mapp had frequently to remind people. The Reverend Kenneth Bartlett's sense of Christian charity had been so distinctly strained by his experience that he had been moved (if the word is not inappropriate, or even insensitive in the circumstances) to dip into the Book of Revelation and take as the text for his sermon the following Sunday 'it was in my mouth sweet as honey: and as soon as I had eaten it my belly was bitter', which Miss Mapp had thought extremely poor taste indeed in a man of the cloth, though she had sat with her usual saintly expression of rapt attention.

By the time the Major finally awoke the sun had already started to dip over the High Street, casting long soft shadows into his bedroom. As he slowly struggled into wakefulness he became aware that one of the long soft shadows was Heather Gillespie, seated in the little armchair he kept in his bedroom, ostensibly for sketching out scenes from his memoirs late at night but in reality for dropping his clothes on to in a very disordered fashion which entirely belied his military upbringing. As she heard him stirring she crossed the room and knelt by the bed. She took one of his rather large paws in a small, cool one of her own and laid the other on his forehead.

'Dear Major,' she said in tones of the softest solicitude. 'How are you feeling?'

The Major admitted that he felt infinitely better for his sleep. As a shaft of light fell upon her face he could not help but notice firstly that Heather close up was even more attractive than she was at a distance of a few feet, and secondly that she seemed to be gazing at him in a rather curious way. Before he could enlarge upon this thought she stood up, saying, 'Well, I'm sure you could do with a nice cup of tea. Why don't you come downstairs, and I'll bring it in to you?'

As she left the room the Major swung his legs off the bed on to the floor. He noticed that his socks and shoes had been removed. So, slightly more worryingly, had his collar and tie. More worrying still, the top two buttons of his trousers had been undone. He had no recollection of any of these things occurring before he had gone to sleep. On the contrary, his impression was that he had fallen upon the bed fully clothed and fully buttoned.

He reflected upon this with some bemusement, manoeuvred his feet into his slippers and went downstairs, where in the space of only a few minutes, it seemed, Heather was on hand with a pot of tea and toast and jam. She poured two cups and sat down opposite him. Perhaps it should have occurred to Major Flint to wonder whether it was entirely appropriate for his housekeeper to be sitting down unbidden to take tea with him, but it did not. On the contrary, it seemed the most natural thing in the world.

'Er, might I enquire ...' he faltered, unsure of exactly how to pose the question.

'Yes, Major, what is it?'

'Well, I mean ... look here, I mean to say ... my clothes, what?'

'I'm sorry, Major, I don't understand. What about your clothes?'

'Well, I have a distinct recollection that I lay down fully clothed. Sloppy, I know, but when a chap is feeling ill he tends just to lie down any old way. Then I woke up ...'

'If you mean your collar and tie and so forth, Major, I took the liberty of removing them to make you more comfortable. You wouldn't want to go to sleep in your collar now, would you? Wake up with an awfully stiff neck, I'll be bound.'

The Major, who had in fact fallen asleep in his collar many times, yes, and woken up with a stiff neck too, could hardly disagree. His fingers strayed to the top button of his trousers, but he decided that this line of enquiry was probably best not pursued.

He discovered that he was ravenously hungry, and crunched down an entire plate of toast with evident relish. Heather brought him another plate, and then some fruitcake, and then a fresh pot of tea. Gradually his intake slowed to more or less normal proportions, and then he stopped altogether and sat back contentedly in his chair. Heather was smiling at him gently, and he realised rather guiltily that he had just indulged in what might be regarded as gluttony, not to mention a rather unexpected burst of appetite for one suffering from a virulent and debilitating tropical disease.

'Afraid I've made rather a pig of myself,' he said with an uneasy laugh.

'Nonsense, Major,' said Heather briskly. 'There's nothing wrong with a man having a healthy appetite. Anyway, it does my heart good to see you eating so well and making such a rapid recovery.'

'Well, it may not do my heart much good,' he replied. 'In fact, I thought I'd put on a bit of weight recently. Must play more golf – been neglecting it a bit, you know.'

'You're a fine figure of a man, Major,' Heather assured him, 'and I shouldn't wonder at it after all those years of action. You must have muscles of steel after wrestling for so long with Pathans, or was it Punjabis? I always get them mixed up.'

The Major was forced to admit that it was difficult not to develop muscles of steel when marching long distances every day with only an encounter with cold steel to look forward to at the end of it. His face set into a stern stare, which reminded Heather awfully of

Douglas Fairbanks gazing heroically into the distance while faced with overwhelming odds.

'You're so lucky, Major,' she sighed. 'And look at me. I have to be very careful what I eat, or I swell up like a balloon.'

'You astonish me!' cried the Major. 'Why, if you'll forgive me saying so, I think your figure is perfection itself. The very epitome of the female form,' he finished in a flourish of sudden inspiration.

Heather demurred. 'You're very kind, Major, and of course I would expect no less from an officer and a gentleman such as you, but surely you must have noticed my legs?'

Major Flint had in fact been gazing at her legs as she spoke, and he started guiltily.

'Your legs? Well, yes … I mean, of course … I mean, one couldn't help but notice them, what? Didn't mean to stare though. Forgive me.'

'There is really nothing to forgive, Major. Unfortunately these new fashions do expose rather a lot of leg, and I have ugly legs. That is the plain truth of it, and it's quite natural that you should stare at them.'

'Ugly?' The Major gawped in genuine stupefaction. 'What on earth are you talking about? They're magnificent.'

'You're very kind, Major, but you really don't have to pretend for my sake. Look at my calves, for instance.'

As it happened, Major Benjy was gazing at her calves intently as she spoke. For the life of him he was unable to see anything wrong with them at all.

'I'm sorry, but this is all quite beyond me,' he said. 'Just what do you think is wrong with your calves exactly?'

'Why, Major,' she cried. 'Surely you can see for yourself. They're fat, that's what, fat.'

'No, no, I won't have that,' he declared emphatically. 'Rounded, yes, Fat, no. Anyway, who wants skinny legs after all, that's what I'd like to know. Women are supposed to be curvy, don't you know.'

Heather Gillespie lifted her skirt a little so that Major Benjy might also pass judgement on her knees and, without really understanding how or why, he found himself paddling across the floor on his knees for a closer examination. He looked up and found that she was gazing at him in that rather curious way again.

The early summer twilight was gathering, and Miss Mapp put down her book with a sigh and retreated from her little secret garden, where she had been sitting very enjoyably with a shawl wrapped around her shoulders against the slight chill of the day. Overhead wheeled the ever-present gulls, crying out to themselves. They were particularly vocal at this time of year, it being their mating and nesting season, but like all Tillingites she never really heard them unless she made a special effort to notice them; in much the same way people who live beside a railway line seem to be able completely to ignore the passing of the Edinburgh sleeper even though the noise and vibration make the windows rattle and the chandelier jump up and down with an altogether charming tinkling sound.

Miss Mapp's mind was greatly troubled by the events of the day. She was certain of what she had heard through the Wyses' window, and while she allowed that she may have woven into her account a teeny amount of dramatic licence she had done so purely for the benefit of her listeners, and not in any way that should have detracted from the basic underlying truth, which was that Major Benjy had behaved very badly and had written Mr Wyse a purported letter of apology which the latter had clearly thought was nonsense. Why, then, had he greeted the Major so effusively when they had next met? It was very puzzling indeed, but she was resolved to get to the bottom of it.

Then there was the business of the cakes. She was quite certain that Evie and Diva had conspired together to push the decision through the meeting in the twinkling of an eye without giving her a fair chance to put forward any of the many valid objections which she would have been able to raise if only she had been allowed the time to think of them. She had been confident of gaining acceptance of her own suggestion for doily-making, a skill which she had been secretly practising for the best part of a year. Now all those pricked fingers and sore thumbs would go for nothing, not to mention the stress of having had to hide all evidence of her activities from casual callers. Many a time had she rushed around stuffing incriminating evidence away under seat cushions, or even into flower vases, while Withers invented some plausible reason to delay a visitor in the hall.

Seated in the garden, her mind had been a swirling maelstrom of creative vindictiveness. At first she had hit upon the idea of copying out exactly the same recipe as Diva had done and producing exactly the same cake. Since it had been agreed that the cakes should be sold afterwards, with the proceeds going to church funds, it had been decided that Mr Wyse should judge the cakes on sight alone. While it was dubious that she could produce a cake that tasted the same as one of Diva's, it should not be beyond her wit to produce one which only looked the same. Faced by two identical cakes, Mr Wyse would surely be unable to award a prize to either one of them, unless he did so jointly, and either outcome would be completely satisfactory to Elizabeth Mapp but entirely unsatisfactory to Godiva Plaistow.

As she had sat and thought a little longer, however, a flaw had appeared in her scheme and she had been forced to rethink her strategy. Fool that she was, she had revealed to Diva in a moment of weakness when she had been provoked beyond endurance that she had seen her copying out the recipe. Miss Mapp and Diva Plaistow had been acquaintances (in the present circumstances she could not bring herself to say 'friends') for many years, and each knew exactly how the other's mind worked. Sitting there now like two players in a game of chess, each would be pondering not just their next move, but their opponent's. Diva, thought Mapp, given the nasty mean-minded person that she was, would surely leap to the conclusion that Miss Mapp would try exactly the sort of Fool's Mate that she did in fact have it in mind to execute. No, clearly some other approach was called for.

As she walked into her garden room and took her usual seat at the window, suddenly it came to her. Mr Wyse was only going to judge the cakes by sight, not taste. Therefore it mattered not how well cooked the cake was, but only how well presented. Diva and Evie were accomplished cooks, and their cakes would appear soft, moist and inviting; she could not compete there. However, she had never known either of them to produce anything with icing on it. Icing, she knew, was a very specialist art indeed, and presumably not one that either lady had ever perfected. Here was a way ahead! Checking the clock, she realised that she could just make it to the library before they closed, and pausing only to put on hat and coat and call to Withers that she was popping out for a few minutes, she sallied forth.

She paused as she saw Irene Coles and Lucy coming down the road towards her. She really had no wish to be drawn into conversation by Irene, since such conversations usually concluded with some gross insult offered by Quaint Irene or, even worse, some curious comment that everyone else obviously found very amusing, since they would cough and shuffle their feet and avoid meeting Miss Mapp's eye, but the point of which was entirely lost on Miss Mapp herself. If there was one thing worse than being insulted, it was being left wondering whether you had been insulted but had been too stupid to realise it.

On this occasion, however, Irene merely took her pipe out of her mouth to shout 'Evening, Mapp', and Lucy gave one of those rare but intense smiles which always made the Major think about a certain lady in Poona many years before, and made Miss Mapp flush with embarrassment anew as she remembered the time she had walked a little too incautiously into Taormina and found Lucy and Irene in a rather advanced state of undress and smearing each other with paints of different colours. It was, as the Major had mused to Mr Wyse one evening in the Trader's Arms, a smile that made you feel as if it could look into your very soul. Mr Wyse, true to form, had said something that could have been French, or Italian, or even Latin, so far as the

Major knew, and looked at him knowingly. Major Benjy had said 'Ah!' deeply and stared significantly into the bottom of his glass.

So Miss Mapp continued on her way, but she had only gone a few yards when a most alarming noise began to make itself heard. It was Major Benjy's voice, no doubt about that. He had a fine singing voice, which Miss Mapp had often admired in church, and for a moment it sounded as if he was indeed trying to burst into song but was having difficulty locating the first note. It was a series of what sounded like 'Ah' but with each successive note rising in tone (perhaps the Major had secretly commenced singing lessons, and was trying out an unusual pentatonic scale?). Starting in the Major's customary rich bass, the series continued for about ten notes, finishing in an undeniably thrilling Verdi baritone on about a top F sharp, but the Major was obviously also experimenting with dynamics, as this last note died away quite quickly, moving from *fortissimo* to *pianissimo* in the space of only two or three seconds. Then there was silence.

To her further puzzlement, Miss Mapp saw Irene and Lucy burst out laughing and then march briskly down the road in military fashion, swinging their arms and getting in step with each other. Irene saluted smartly as Lucy opened the front door and then they vanished inside Taormina, further sounds of hilarity emanating from within it.

Miss Mapp sighed deeply and continued on her way with a little shake of her head, adding yet one more unexplained item to her list of very curious events that had occurred that day.

Chapter 5

The next day dawned bright and fair and Miss Mapp, seated at her usual morning vantage point, would have felt that God was in his heaven and all was right with the world, had she not been highly perplexed by not one but two puzzling incidents from the day before, as well as deeply wounded by the domestic duel affair.

Mr Wyse was known far and wide for his intelligence and erudition. Why, then, should he apparently have fallen hook line and sinker for such a transparent lie on the Major's part? It must have been clear to anyone who had eyes to see with that the Major had been three sheets to the wind, and had in fact disgraced himself even more comprehensively than on any previous occasion.

Even if he had fallen for it, or pretended to out of politeness, that still did not explain him having jumped quite voluntarily out of the car and greeting the Major in such effusive fashion. A friendly wave through the window would have sufficed. She mused a little longer on this weighty conundrum, and then gave up.

Yet there was still the question of the extraordinary noises emanating from the Major's house the previous evening. What on earth was one to make of that? Again, she grappled with the problem for some time and then gave up. However, it had all clearly meant something to Irene and Lucy, indeed it had occasioned them much amusement. She resolved to get to the bottom of the matter, no matter how long it took her.

At that very moment, as if telepathic impulses had been buzzing backwards and forwards between the two houses, the Major emerged from his front door, and Miss Mapp instantly noticed three things that were very odd about this. First, it was a good hour or so before the Major, who was notorious for oversleeping ('Sleeping it off, more like,' Miss Mapp muttered darkly to herself) normally saw the light of day.

Secondly, he was in company with Heather Gillespie. With the exception of the Wyses' chauffeur, no Tillingite went shopping with their servants. It would have been intolerable to them to have them hanging around, wasting their time, while their masters and mistresses swapped the important news of the day, and unthinkable that one should not be free to trade gossip as one wished, for fear of it being overheard; '*Pas devant les domestiques*,' as Miss Mapp was apt to hiss authoritatively on such occasions.

Thirdly, and most puzzling of all, it was the Major who was holding the shopping basket. Naturally, had he been accompanying a female member of his family, or a friend such as Miss Mapp who also happened to be female, it would have been the most natural thing in the world for him to carry their basket. Indeed, onlookers would have been rightly aghast had he not done so. Yet here he was in company with his servant and it was clearly she who was the right person to carry the basket, not him.

So here was yet another mystery to solve, and Miss Mapp felt it her clear public duty to resolve all and any mysteries concerning other Tilling residents, regardless of what embarrassment might be caused by her pulling into the glare of public scrutiny matters which others might have been eager not to see the light of day. No, it was her duty and she was resolute in its execution. She watched as, to her surprise, the Major and Mrs Gillespie turned right at the Wyses' house and headed towards Curfew Street. The shops all lay in the opposite direction; that way there was nothing other than the Norman Tower and the Gun Garden. Aflame with curiosity, she hastened to fetch her hat and shopping basket and set out to follow them.

As she reached Curfew Street, she glanced right and left. Nobody was in sight to the right, where the Viewpoint Terrace stretched for some distance. It was therefore much more likely that, as she had surmised, the pair had taken the shorter route to the left that curved round to the Gun Garden in front of the Norman Tower. With the scent of her prey now growing stronger in her nostrils with every moment that passed, she waddled doggedly in pursuit.

As she rounded the bend and stood before the tower, at the top of the shallow flight of steps that led down to the old gun platform, she espied the Major and Mrs Gillespie standing very close together, looking out across the marshes towards the sea. So closely, in fact, that they might almost have been touching – but no, surely she must be mistaken. Infuriatingly, she could not hear what they were saying so she tiptoed down the steps in an effort to get a little closer. However, the Major, no doubt with an instinct drawn from many a tiger hunt, looked around and saw her.

'Ah,' he said.

Miss Mapp now saw that she must have been mistaken, as the Major and Mrs Gillespie were not standing in close proximity to each other at all. Unless, of course the Major had cunningly moved to one side as he swivelled to greet her? While still pondering this possibility, Miss Mapp realised that it was necessary for her to say something. Not to explain her unusual and unexplained presence in the Gun Garden, of course, nor to refute any as yet unspoken suspicion that she might have been following them, but certainly to say something, if only for the sake of common politeness.

'Major Benjy,' she cooed, fixing him with one of her sweetest smiles. 'Out and about early today, I see.'

Her gaze switched to Heather Gillespie, and she hoped that the smile lost none of its sweetness.

'I don't think we've met?' she ventured.

'Forgive me, forgive me,' said the Major quickly. 'Miss Mapp, may I introduce Mrs Gillespie, my new housekeeper.'

'How do you do, Miss Mapp,' said Heather politely, while Miss Mapp murmured 'Charmed' while increasing the fixed sweetness of her smile still more, were such a thing possible.

'I trust you will be happy in Tilling, Gillespie,' said Miss Mapp. 'Such a quiet little place, you know.'

'Oh, I'm sure I will be very happy here, thank you, miss,' replied Heather, 'and as for quiet places, I positively relish them. With such a wonderful gentleman as Major Flint to look after, I am sure my time here will be a real joy.'

'Indeed, let us hope so,' echoed Miss Mapp with every appearance of sincerity. She knew that there was something that was troubling her, and suddenly she remembered what it was.

'Ah yes,' she said, 'I knew there was something I wanted to ask you, Major.'

Major Benjy eyed her warily.

'I was out for a walk yesterday evening just as it was starting to get dark, and I couldn't help overhearing you making the most unusual noises. I thought perhaps you might have started taking singing lessons secretly, though really I don't know what such a fine singer as you would want with lessons.'

'Ah, no, indeed,' said the Major breezily, with what he hoped was a modest chuckle. 'Singing lessons, eh? The very idea!'

Miss Mapp returned to the attack. In the meantime Heather Gillespie had turned aside and was studying one of the cannons very intently, while coughing quietly into her handkerchief. Perhaps she was consumptive? Miss Mapp found the thought comforting, and stored it away for further consideration.

'That's exactly what I thought, Major, no need of singing lessons. So why the exercises, or scales, or whatever they were? Dear neighbours though we are, I don't think I would want to suffer that sort of noise every evening.'

Heather Gillespie seemed quickly to master her coughing fit, and broke into the conversation.

'If you'll excuse me, Miss Mapp, I think I can explain matters quite easily.'

'You?' Miss Mapp deigned to acknowledge her presence, but with the air of a house prefect sending his fag to warm a lavatory seat.

'Yes, Miss Mapp,' replied Heather evenly. 'You see, the noise you heard was the Major crying out in pain. I'm sure he's too modest and gentlemanly to mention it himself, but that is in fact what it was.'

'But, dear Major Benjy,' cried Miss Mapp in an excess of solicitude, 'you poor man. What on earth were you suffering, that you were moved to cry out in such a way?'

The Major seemed about to reply two or three times, and then cleared his throat in exactly the way a man might who needed time to think of a reply.

'The culprit was none other than myself, I fear, Miss Mapp,' explained Heather. 'You see, my aunt always swore by a hot bread poultice in the case of any fever, and that's what I was applying to Major Flint's back. Very hot, it was, you see, and that's when he cried out.'

'Sorry you were disturbed, Miss Elizabeth,' said the Major with the air of one who has nobly borne great suffering. 'I will try to bear the pain with more stoicism next time. Why, I remember once having an old lead musket ball cut out of me by the surgeon in the Punjab …'

Miss Mapp's face bore witness to the inner struggle of a deeply suspicious soul who is struggling to assimilate unexpected information. The conflict was brief; suspicion emerged victorious, and swept away the Punjabi musket ball.

'Bread poultice?' she queried, with furrowed eyebrows. 'I've never heard of that being a cure for fever.'

'Oh, but it is, Miss Elizabeth, or should I say it was, for it certainly did the trick with me. No fever at all today. Completely restored to health.'

'Hm,' said Miss Mapp, who had her own decided ideas about the nature of the Major's illness, but decided with unusual discretion that now was not the appropriate time to air them. 'Then it is fortunate indeed that you have Gillespie to look after you.'

'Bless you, Miss Mapp, it's really no trouble at all. Why, a fine gentleman like the Major, it's a positive treat to look after him. He does enjoy his food so.'

'And long may it continue, say I,' broke in the Major. 'You should have seen my breakfast this morning, Miss Elizabeth, and the cakes at teatime – oh!' He broke off with a little gurgle of appreciation.

This mention of cakes reminded Miss Mapp that she had other challenges to meet that day.

'That's splendid, dear Major Benjy,' she said, fixing him with her gaze and ignoring his companion completely. 'It does my heart good to know that you are eating properly again. Well, *au reservoir*, then. I'll see you at Diva's for tea, of course.'

'Of course.' The Major raised his cap and beamed after her. He was in a mood to beam at anyone today, even that damned paper boy who either gave him the wrong paper altogether, left it outside in the rain to get wet or stuffed it into the letter box in such a way as to tear it to unreadable shreds.

Miss Mapp made her way towards the shops with a worried tread. She had the infuriating feeling that she was missing out on something and, more importantly, something which, if only she could properly understand it, could well be to the detriment of another member of Tilling society. What had Irene and Lucy found so amusing? And was it possible that that wretched Gillespie woman had been laughing as well in the Gun Garden just now?

However, she did not have long to occupy herself with such thoughts, vexing though they were, as it was but a short walk from the old gun platform to Twemlow's, the grocer, and she pulled out her shopping list as she entered. It turned out that icing sugar was ruinously dear, and though she claimed several times to Mrs Twemlow that she could buy it more cheaply in Hastings, both Mrs Twemlow and the price remained unmoved. It was also surprisingly heavy, and but for the fact that she wanted to get it home as quickly as possible and before anyone else had a chance to remark upon her purchases, Twemlow's having been briefly and mercifully empty during her visit, she would have left it at the shop and had Withers call for it later. As it was, she had to stroll home with every appearance of nonchalance when in fact her basket was becoming heavier by the minute, and by the time she reached Mallards she strongly suspected that she had given herself tennis elbow – all for the dubious pleasure of being able to launch her icing skills upon an unsuspecting Tilling.

She dropped her basket on the kitchen table with a sigh of relief and flexed her aching arm. Withers took the *Tilling Gazette* from the top of the basket and looked up askance.

'Why, miss,' she said, 'what on earth are we wanting with so much icing sugar?'

'Mum's the word, Withers, if you don't mind,' replied her mistress briskly. 'I am going to produce an iced cake for the Spring Show, but nobody else is to know about it, if you please.'

'Oh, miss!,' cried Withers in obvious admiration. 'What an idea! Nobody round here goes in for icing, I know that for a fact. Not Mrs Plaistow, nor the vicar's wife neither.'

'Exactly, Withers,' responded Tilling's master strategist crisply, 'and that is why Mallards will bring home the bacon, or the rosette or whatever it is. Now mind you say nothing to anybody; the honour of Mallards is at stake.'

'Don't you worry none about that, miss,' Withers assured her. She was still lost in admiration for the scale of what Miss Mapp was attempting. Since she had iced a cake before and Miss Mapp had not, her mistress might have done well to pause for thought and reflect on just why Withers was so impressed with the scale of her undertaking, but self-doubt was not a luxury which Miss Mapp allowed herself.

'What a lark, miss!' cried Withers.

'Yes, Withers, a lark indeed,' replied Elizabeth Mapp complacently.

The first part of the master plan required her actually to produce a cake; after all, should there be no cake there would be nothing to ice. She had actually had the unworthy thought of venturing into Hastings or Brighton and purchasing a fruitcake, but the fear of possible discovery on the train, or while walking from the station, had persuaded her that honesty was the best policy. After all, she reasoned, Mr Wyse was not going to taste the cake, or even cut into it, so what lay underneath the icing was largely irrelevant. It could even have been a cardboard box. Now there was an idea! But no, she abandoned it reluctantly. The cake was to be sold afterwards, and her stratagem would be discovered by the innocent purchaser, who would obviously lose no time in spreading the story all over town.

Miss Mapp therefore laboured mightily and succeeded after some hours in producing a serviceable fruitcake mix just as it was time to set off for Wasters, Diva Paistow's house. Calling to Withers to take it out when it was done, she put it in the oven and hastened out to tea.

It was but a short walk, and as she strolled past first the fishmonger and then the greengrocer, Miss Mapp's heart was light. First there was the matter of the cake. She was confident that she had comprehensively outsmarted Diva. Diva, being both predictable and of limited intelligence, would undoubtedly assume that she, Elizabeth, would attempt to imitate her chocolate cake and would thus be unable to play what was probably her strongest card. Miss Mapp's iced confection, on the other hand, would fall upon the Spring Show like a bolt from the blue and sweep all (well, Mr Wyse at least) before it. Secondly, there was another secret which she was planning to reveal during the afternoon, but for the moment she hugged it to herself, relishing the fact that, as usual, she currently enjoyed a significant moral advantage over her fellows.

So light was her heart, in fact, that she found herself calling out spontaneously and cheerily to Irene Coles, who had just come out of the stationer's shop.

'Ah, good afternoon, quaint one! Tea at Diva's, of course?'

Quaint Irene looked understandably shocked at this sudden amity.

'Hello, Mapp, what are you looking so cheerful about? Been at the cooking sherry, have we?'

Miss Mapp ignored this provocation.

'No use, Irene, dearest. You will absolutely not succeed in denting my good humour this afternoon.'

Irene gazed at her suspiciously.

'If you're in a good mood it can only be because something awful has happened to someone else ...'

'Tra la la,' trilled Miss Mapp with girlish glee.

'I know!' exclaimed Irene. 'You've found out something dreadful about someone and you're savouring the thought of making sure everyone else finds out about it.'

Miss Mapp said 'Tra la la' again, but this time a little more determinedly, since Irene was getting uncomfortably close to the truth. Fortunately they were now outside Wasters, and their brief exchange drew to a natural conclusion.

The door was on the latch, as was the custom in Tilling, and Miss Mapp most unusually stood back to allow Quaint Irene to precede her into Wasters. It was not a large house, and the hallway was particularly narrow, so as Irene turned left into the living room (which Diva had once or twice thought of opening to the public as a tea room) Miss Mapp was able to turn right into the kitchen unobserved. Her twitching nostrils caught the scent of something cooking, and it was the work of a moment to turn the oven knob from mark five to mark nine before slipping back into the hall and following Irene into Diva's front room. In fact, since Irene had been wearing a broad-rimmed hat which hid anyone behind her from view, and since she had lingered on the threshold for a moment with a cheery 'What-ho, Tilling!', Miss Mapp's undercover activities in the kitchen passed entirely unobserved.

The Bartletts were already present, as was Major Benjy, and the first pot of tea had already been expended. Diva said 'Shan't be a tick' and slipped past them in search of more hot water. Miss Mapp held her breath for a moment, but all was well. Diva was clearly preoccupied by the kettle on the hob, and the ejaculation of horror and dismay which Miss Mapp had feared did not manifest itself. Better still, once Diva returned to the room she at once seated herself on the sofa, so there seemed no immediate danger of Miss Mapp's *ruse de guerre* being discovered.

'Thank you so much, dear,' she said, as she took the proffered cup of tea from Diva. She surveyed the plate of biscuits, selected a chocolate digestive, and bit into it with relish.

'So tell me, dear Mrs Padre,' she gushed, 'what wonderful creation have you decided upon for the Spring Show?'

It was an affectation entirely of her own making to address Mrs Bartlett as 'Mrs Padre', and the object of the salutation had in fact on many occasions begged Miss Mapp to call her 'Evie', but because Miss Mapp was the perpetrator it was tolerated, though it had never been widely adopted in the same way, for example, as '*au reservoir*'.

Evie Bartlett squeaked rather inaudibly through a mouthful of custard cream, and her husband came to the rescue.

'Now then, Mistress Mapp, ye would'nae want to spoil the surprise, would ye? After all, we have only to wait until the morrow for all to be revealed, ye ken.'

'Quite,' said Diva emphatically. 'Much the best thing.'

Darkness suddenly fell upon the room as a large motor car pulled up outside the window, signalling the arrival of the Wyses. The four new arrivals – Mr and Mrs Wyse, the Contessa and Isabel – stretched the proportions of Diva's living room to their limit, particularly as Susan was wearing a large fur coat which took up almost as much room as another person. Mr Wyse perched delicately on the arm of his wife's chair, charmingly attempting to alleviate the cramped seating requirements as much as possible.

'Oh dear,' said Diva, 'I keep forgetting that we normally only ever have eight people in here, and that's with all the furniture taken out and two bridge tables instead.'

'Now do not worry yourself on our account, Mrs Plaistow,' said the Contessa in her usual stentorian tones. 'It is extremely kind of you to invite us into your charming home.'

'Hear, hear, Amelia,' said Mr Wyse promptly, sparking a general murmur of Tillingites wishing to associate themselves with the Contessa's views. Miss Mapp stirred her tea with a detached air and said nothing.

'I have always envied you this room, Diva,' said Susan Wyse from somewhere within her fur coat. 'So well-proportioned.'

'Exactly! Delightful!' duetted her husband.

'And as for being a wee thing snug,' proffered the Padre, 'why, what can that distress folk when they are with bonny friends?'

This brought forth a general 'Ah!' of agreement and appreciation, which emboldened the Padre to continue.

'Why, I well remember taking tea one day with my uncle the bishop when there were fourteen of us gathered in his wee study.'

'Why, Padre!' Miss Mapp cooed. 'I never knew there was a bishop in your family.'

'Only a colonial bishop, ye ken,' demurred the Reverend Bartlett, 'a cousin on my mother's side.' He stirred his tea contemplatively. 'Uncle Septimus to me, but Bishop of Matabeleland to the kirk. And, of course, not exactly in the family any more. He went to heaven some years ago, God bless the man.'

Major Benjy, who had been exhibiting the air of somebody who is not paying attention to the conversation, suddenly said 'Ah!' loudly enough to arouse Miss Mapp's suspicions that he had been imbibing something stronger than Darjeeling. 'That's where the Davenports went.'

He became aware that the others were gazing blankly at him and so he elucidated. 'You know, that couple who took Mallards a few summers back. Nice folk, I thought, though he was a bit mean with the bottle, and she was a bit scrawny, particularly around the ...' He became aware that the conversation was headed in a rather indelicate direction and said 'Ah' again, but this time in his 'Ladies present' tone of voice.

Miss Mapp broke the somewhat baffled silence.

'Are you quite sure, Major dear? I never heard anything about it.'

'Oh, yes, definitely. Tiverton or somewhere, I think.'

'That's Devon, Major,' said Miss Mapp coldly, in the manner of a schoolmistress who has found a boy dozing at the back of the class. 'We were talking about Heaven. Different place entirely, I'm sure you will agree.'

'Oh, yes. Quite,' averred Benjy hurriedly, and after a few seconds said 'Quite' again, just to lend emphasis to his level of agreement.

A slightly awkward pause ensued, which was broken predictably by Mr Wyse.

'At least Heaven will not be claiming you for a while, Major. I am glad to see that you seem to have made such a speedy recovery from your bilharzia.' He executed a small bow in the direction of the reprieved man.

'Ah, yes, bilharzia,' said Miss Mapp firmly. Such was the hint of menace in her voice that everyone gazed at her, wondering what was coming next.

'You know, Major,' she said sweetly, 'I always thought it was India where you served king and country.'

'Quite right, dear lady,' averred the Major. 'India it was, indeed.'

'Then perhaps you could enlighten us,' continued Miss Mapp in honeyed tones, 'how it is that you managed to contract a disease that is confined entirely to Africa?'

A further awkward pause ensued. Mr Wyse's eyes met those of the Padre as both struggled to think of an interjection that might deflect Miss Mapp from her grim purpose. Fortunately, the Major responded before the pause become too unbearable.

'Ah, now, funny thing is I did actually go to Africa – on the way back from India. The boat touched at Mombasa and I spent a whole day ashore. A few hours after I got back on board I was taken ill, and the old sawbones they had on the boat diagnosed it as bilharzia. Clearest case he'd ever seen, apparently.'

'Well now, there we are,' crooned the Padre in conciliatory tones. 'The mystery is solved. Now, what about this wee bakery duel, eh, ladies?'

Miss Mapp was not to be deflected so easily.

'You went swimming, then, I presume, Major?' she asked, fixing him with a rather dangerous smile.

'Swimming?' he echoed incredulously. 'I had bilharzia, madam. I was very sick. Added to which,' he went on, 'I distinctly recollect that the boat had no swimming pool.'

'In Mombasa, I meant. Before you got back on the boat.'

The Major gave the disarming chuckle of a well-travelled man.

'Dear lady,' he said, 'to go swimming off the beach at Mombasa is to risk almost certain death. I understand that just about every shark in the Indian Ocean makes a beeline for the place. Only the week before I was there an officer from the Askaris dashed into the waves to rescue a chap from a shark. Managed to get him out, but minus his legs. Bled to death right there on the beach, poor chap.'

Evie Bartlett, who was well known for her delicate stomach, gave a spontaneous cry of dismay, and even Mr Wyse was moved to say, 'Dear, dear, most unfortunate. Poor fellow.'

'So you didn't go swimming at all, then?' persisted Miss Mapp. 'Not even in a lake or a river or anything?'

'I most certainly did not,' said the Major emphatically. 'I bought the assegai and knobkerrie which now stand in my hallway, and then had a few beers with some brother officers. You have to, you know, out there, I mean. The heat.'

'That really is most curious,' said Miss Mapp with an even more dangerous smile as she prepared to deliver the *coup de grâce* with relish. 'You see, the only way in which you can possibly catch bilharzia is by swimming or washing in infected water.'

She savoured the ensuing silence. Only she knew that there was yet more to come.

'And the disease is not recurrent.'

Collapse of stout party, she thought triumphantly. However, her resoluteness of character rendered it impossible to refrain from kicking a man while he was down, and she decided to air her encyclopaedic (literally, since it emanated from the library's *Encyclopaedia Britannica*) knowledge of the subject.

'There have to be snails in the water, you see. And not just any old snails, either. These are a special type of snail that harbour a special type of worm. The worms get inside your body and go all around in your bloodstream, multiplying as they go.'

At this point little ejaculations of dismay and disgust were uttered and Evie Bartlett looked distinctly queasy, but Miss Mapp pressed on regardless.

'They eat away at your organs, you see, particularly the liver and the kidneys, I understand. That's why it can never be recurrent, of course. Either you get rid of the worms or you die. Eaten by worms from the inside.'

She savoured the last six words, uttering them slowly and ruminatively. This, however, was altogether too much for most of the party. Evie Bartlett ran out of the room suddenly with her hand over her mouth and could be heard retching loudly a few moments later, while her husband vanished, doubtless to assist her. Diva put her cup down very firmly on her saucer and said, 'Really, Elizabeth!'

'Miss Mapp,' said Mr Wyse very gravely, 'with all due respect, I really must insist that we change the subject. This one is hardly seemly for tea party conversation.'

Being rebuked by Mr Wyse was rather like being savaged by a koala bear, but a definite rebuke it was nonetheless. Perhaps disturbed at the prospect of being seen to be in any breach of etiquette himself, he adroitly swung the conversation in a different direction.

'For my part,' he said, 'I find I am indebted to Major Flint.'

Another half bow from a seated position was executed in the Major's direction. 'You see, it was his intervention that allowed me to finish my crossword. Bilharzia was the answer to the one clue I simply couldn't get. Wretchedly bad clue it was, in my opinion. I'd been sweating over it for simply ages. Susan couldn't get it either.'

So that was it, thought Miss Mapp. Suddenly the scene she had witnessed through the Wyse's window made sense. No wonder she had got the wrong end of the stick, though, given the ridiculous nature of the Major's excuse. How like a man! Mr Wyse had been offered a heaven-sent opportunity to make one of his fellow Tillingites look ridiculous and had spurned it, all because his pride had been flattered by being able to finish his crossword.

'Ah, yes, often the way, you know,' said the Major brightly. 'Why, many's the time I've wrestled with a crossword for hours, only to see the answer the next day and curse myself for a damned fool, pardon my French.'

Miss Mapp, who was well aware that the Major's attention span for even the *Daily Telegraph* crossword was limited by the time it took to finish his second morning pot of tea, felt her irritation with the whole situation threatening to boil over. Why, she had exposed Major Benjy completely as an utter charlatan right there in Diva's living room in front of everybody, yet they all seemed determined to ignore her revelation. She had looked forward to savouring his disgrace, perhaps to Mr Wyse's pained expression as he put down his cup of tea and apologised gravely to Diva for having to leave, perhaps even to Quaint Irene's uncontrolled cackles of mirth, yet seemingly as far as they were all concerned there was nothing worth savouring.

Diva could be heard in the hallway, shepherding the Bartletts out of the front door.

'So sorry, dear,' she was saying, 'hope you feel better soon. Perhaps a little oatmeal when you get home, just to settle the stomach?'

The Padre was heard to remark that they had been anticipating liver and kidneys that evening, but that perhaps the wee wifie would be able to rustle up some bread and cheese instead.

'Liver and kidneys indeed!' exclaimed Diva as she shut the door.

She bustled into the room, gazing reproachfully at Miss Mapp.

'Surely you remember, Elizabeth, that Evie has a particularly delicate digestion? You would do well to remember what your famous marrow jam did to her.'

Miss Mapp gasped in outraged surprise.

'It was greengage, as you well know,' she spluttered, 'and there was nothing wrong with it. Nothing at all! If dear Padre and Evie were ill that week it was all a ghastly coincidence, that's all.'

Mr Wyse looked pained. 'Dear ladies …' he began, but Major Benjy broke in with a stout defence of Miss Mapp's preserve-making abilities.

'Ah, no, Mrs Plaistow, say what you will, Miss Elizabeth is a master jam-maker. Why, I had some of her chutney with some cold meat only a few evenings ago, and it was quite delicious.'

'Really?' enquired Quaint Irene innocently. 'I thought it was marmalade you said she'd given you. You gave one jar to me, and it certainly said "marmalade" on the label, though I admit it looked and smelt more like chutney when I opened it.'

Miss Mapp gave Irene a look that spoke volumes.

'I do think we can all accept that the dear Major is capable of telling the difference between chutney and marmalade, Irene,' she said in a tone of voice which combined the infinite patience required when addressing a backward child with a definite hint of menace.

'So am I!' retorted Irene, entirely unabashed, 'and I certainly wouldn't have thought of putting any of it on my toast.'

Perhaps fortunately, in view of where the conversation appeared to be heading, Isabel suddenly stood up, sniffed loudly and said, 'I say! Can anyone smell burning?'

Diva gave a scream and ran from the room. The others trooped after her and gathered in a helpless little huddle in the hallway as she threw open the oven, releasing a cloud of black smoke. She snatched up the oven gloves, pulled something out and dumped it in the sink.

'What is it, Diva?' asked Susan Wyse. 'Not ...' She stopped and gave a gasp of horror. 'It's surely not your cake for tomorrow?'

'No, thank goodness,' replied Diva. 'To tell the truth I haven't started that yet – I was going to make it this evening so it's nice and fresh for the morning. No, this was just some braised beef I was stewing for my supper. I can't understand how the oven came to be turned up like that. I'm usually so careful.'

She gazed around the kitchen in puzzlement as if the answer would suddenly present itself on a shelf, or hanging on a hook.

'Easily done, I'm sure, dear,' murmured Miss Mapp. 'Well, *au reservoir* then, everybody.' So saying she flapped a hand in the general direction of the kitchen and slipped out of the front door.

'Well, at least it wasn't your cake, old thing,' said Irene, 'so you'll still be able to give Mapp one in the eye tomorrow.' She turned to leave and suddenly paused on the threshold and exclaimed: 'I say!'

'What?' chorused the Wyse party.

'No, surely not. Surely even Mapp wouldn't sink that low.'

'What on earth do you mean, Miss Coles?' asked Mr Wyse.

'Well, I remember distinctly now that when I came in Mapp was with me and she insisted, positively insisted, mind, that I should go in first. She would have had time just to slip into the kitchen quickly, you know, and if she thought that it was Diva's cake that was in the oven then all she had to do was give the knob a quick tweak and come out again as if nothing had happened.'

'Miss Coles,' said the Major stiffly, 'I am sure you will understand that I cannot remain here while you blacken the name of Miss Elizabeth. Goodbye, Mrs Plaistow. Thank you for my tea.'

The Major strode off while the Wyse party looked at each other uncomfortably, said their goodbyes and followed the Major out into the road. As they looked back, Irene and Diva could be seen through the kitchen window, locked in animated discussion. Mr Wyse glanced up the road and waved an immaculately gloved hand for the Rolls Royce.

'I cannot believe,' protested Susan Wyse a trifle feebly, 'that Elizabeth would stoop to such a thing.'

'That woman,' said the Contessa very decisively indeed, 'is capable of anything. Anything! I really think she is the most dreadful woman I have ever met. I trust that whoever is judging this wretched cake competition will bear her conduct in mind.'

She glanced meaningfully at her brother as she followed Susan's fur coat into the capacious interior of the car.

'I'm sure he will keep a completely open mind, Amelia, as I'm sure everybody would wish,' he said blandly.

Chapter 6

The next morning saw frenzied cake-making activities occurring in various kitchens around Tilling with varying degrees of success and satisfaction. The occupants of both Mallards and Wasters, however, found they had quite unexpectedly arrived at the bottom end of their range of expectations. Each had genuinely expected their efforts to be crowned with success, yet each had been cruelly disappointed.

Diva Plaistow was indeed a talented cook, and would have backed herself to turn out a cake with prize-winning potential ninety-nine times out of a hundred. Unfortunately this seemed to be that one-hundredth random observation that bedevils statistical sampling.

'Fool, Godiva, fool!' she hissed to herself as she sadly surveyed the ruination of all her hopes. 'You should have tried out the recipe first. Whoever would rely on a completely new recipe for an important occasion like this? Only an idiot like you, that's who!'

It may seem to the innocent observer that Diva was being unduly harsh with herself, but her pride was at stake and she imagined with horror the scene which would unfold at the church hall when she was forced to admit that she had messed up the cake she was making and consequently had nothing to enter for the domestic duel. How smug Elizabeth Mapp would be! How loud would be her protestations of sympathy and dismay, yet how insincere. Perhaps she could pretend that she had in fact produced an outstanding cake but had dropped it on the floor, or sat on it by mistake, or seen it carried off by gulls while cooling on the windowsill? No. Elizabeth would never believe such a story, even if it were true, and would see to it that nobody else did either.

Rarely had Diva felt so totally wretched. She stood and gazed morosely at the disappointing mess sitting in the middle of her kitchen table. If it had been a chocolate crown, moulded in a cake tin, there might have been some excuse for its appearance. The outer two-thirds of the cake looked magnificent, but the inner third had collapsed completely, sagging rather like the apple pie that Evie Bartlett had produced a few weeks ago, having forgotten to insert the rather charming crust support in the shape of a blackbird which she usually employed. If only some sort of support had been available to put inside her cake …

It was while thus idly musing that her glance chanced upon a tin of black Cherry Blossom boot polish sitting in the shoe-cleaning box in the corner of the room. She gave a little cry of wonder and pounced upon it. Bringing it over to the table, she realised with a surge of excitement that it was exactly the right size. She carefully scooped out the fallen centre of the cake, placed the round tin in place, and smoothed the rogue cake pieces over the top of it. She stood back and evaluated it dubiously. It might look all right from a distance, but close investigation would be bound to raise suspicions, not least because you could see the outline of the tin in places showing through the thin covering of cake. Again her gaze wandered around the kitchen and this time it alighted upon a bag of icing sugar. It was the work of but a few moments to give the cake a thick dusting. This time when she stepped back it was with a gasp of satisfaction. Not only was the tin now completely unnoticeable, but the cake looked truly magnificent. She went in search of her hat, with a spring in her step and a song in her heart.

It was as she was humming to herself and adjusting her hat in front of the mirror that the inherent flaw in her hitherto brilliant plan began to percolate through her good humour. The cake might look wonderful, but it was going to be bought by some poor wretch, and it certainly would not taste wonderful. In fact, whoever bought it would discover all too quickly and easily the depths to which she had been prepared to stoop to cover up her own ineptitude. Suppose it was Elizabeth who cut into it! Her blood ran cold at the thought.

She stood in front of the mirror for some seconds, staring fixedly back at herself as she tried to think out some new variation of her plan. Suddenly she hit upon it. All that was needed was for someone to buy her cake the moment the show opened; someone nominated by herself, that is, and who could be trusted not to enquire too closely into the finer details. Normally her thoughts would have turned instantly to Mr Wyse, whose gentlemanly instincts would of course prevent him from intervening in any affair which a lady wished to be kept confidential, but he was due to judge the cake competition and would therefore be hopelessly compromised. No, it would have to be Irene.

She wrapped the cake and the cardboard base she had cut for it in brown paper, and hurried off to the church hall. There were as yet only a few people hanging around, and nobody she knew. There was a table which had clearly been set aside for the cakes, as one or two had already been deposited. Spread out across the front of the table were a number of little paper flags with ladies' names on them; Evie's work, presumably. Diva unwrapped her cake very carefully, stuck the 'Mrs Plaistow' flag delicately into it, and went in search of Irene Coles.

Taormina appeared uninhabited, but she gave a loud bang with the knocker just to make sure. This produced sounds of movement from within, and shortly Lucy opened the door dressed in jodhpurs and riding boots. Irene, it transpired, had already departed for some morning sketching on the marshes, and the time of her reappearance was uncertain. With some trepidation, therefore, Diva hesitantly confided her mission to Lucy instead, who thankfully accepted it cheerfully without asking any questions whatsoever. She was just off to exercise a friend's horse near Winchelsea, but would be back around noon. With the show opening at two, she would have plenty of time in hand. She would be standing by the cake table a few minutes in advance, and the moment the Mayor declared the proceedings open she would pounce on the cake with Diva's name on it. However puzzled she may have been by Diva's plea to throw the cake away unsampled and, if possible, without anyone seeing it, her reaction was of one who is asked to undertake such missions on a regular basis.

In Mallards, meanwhile, Miss Mapp's hopes had similarly been undone. The cake itself had emerged fairly solidly and unexcitingly from its baking tin the evening before, but the whole exercise of icing it had proved quite beyond her. When she twisted paper into a cone, filled it with icing and squeezed it as her book indicated, the icing oozed out in all directions, and chiefly over Miss Mapp herself. When the cake was finally covered in an irregular layer the kitchen table and floor were liberally coated with at least three times as much; indeed, it convincingly resembled the sort of snowy nativity scene which she was so fond of creating at Christmas. In desperation she gave up and went to bed, leaving Withers to clear up the mess and trusting to a good night's sleep to revive her own creative abilities.

Sadly, however, Hypnos was of no assistance on this occasion and Miss Mapp's efforts, which grew increasingly desperate as the deadline approached, succeeding in producing only something which closely resembled a child's first efforts with modelling clay rendered as a snowscape. Her intention to reproduce Tilling church in its square complete with tower and vicarage she realised, alas too late, had probably always been an over-ambitious project. She had never succeeded in raising the tower, while the church itself was little more than an indeterminate lump slightly larger than the others.

She paused to consider her options. Like the inhabitant of Wasters at the other end of the street, she mulled over the possibility of tripping over in the street with a little cry of dismay, and hurling her precious cargo viciously into the cobbles as she did so. The prospect was appealing, not least because of the universal sympathy which such a calamity was sure to arouse, but the more she pondered, the less she liked it. While the bulk of Tilling would doubtless be too good-natured to believe that anything other than sad mischance had precipitated her tumble, there were some evil spirits abroad – Diva and Quaint Irene to name but two – who would be sure to express regret to her face but launch the most vile rumours and insinuations behind her back. While she had weathered such calumny in the past and would doubtless be forced to do so again in the future, she had no wish to bring such an event about unnecessarily, particularly as she was growing a little unsettled about the constancy of Major Benjy's support, normally her rock at such times. No, there had to be another way.

The problem was that the only other alternative was deeply unappealing. She could see no option but to take her cake to the church hall and brazen the affair out. Yet how her face would burn with embarrassment while the assembled ladies of Tilling gathered around the cake table all afternoon and tittered at the ruination of all her hopes and plans, for one thing was certain: nobody would even dream of buying her sad wreck of a cake and so it would lie there all afternoon, cruelly exposed to public ridicule. Unless …

Miss Mapp stood transfixed as a sudden brainwave took hold of her. Why should nobody buy her cake? Why should somebody, somebody carefully nominated by her, of course, not buy her cake the very moment that the show opened? That way nobody need ever get to see it at all, apart from Mr Wyse of course and anybody else who might happen to see it while it was awaiting judgment.

She sat down with a strong cup of tea to try to think things through as calmly as she could. She could perhaps minimise the chance of casual observation by arriving at the church hall right at the moment of judging. Mr Wyse always insisted on being in the room alone on these occasions, so she might well be able to rush in, full of apologies, and put the cake on the table, completely unseen by anyone other than him. As for Mr Wyse himself, he would of course be witness to her disgrace, but the one quality of his on which everybody was agreed they could absolutely rely was his discretion. No matter what his private thoughts might be, he would never divulge a word to a soul, particularly where the interests of a lady were concerned. There would still be the matter of his quizzical glance to endure, but she reasoned that this was a small price to pay, given the even greater awfulness of the other possibilities.

She glanced up at her mother's clock and saw that, if she was to delay her entry as she intended, she still had a good half hour to spare before her dramatic dash down the road sounding rather like the White Rabbit in *Alice in Wonderland*, shouting, 'Oh dear! Oh dear! I shall be too late!' to anyone she happened to see. She put down her cup and saucer with a determined air and went to be deeply unpleasant to her gardener for twenty minutes or so, which revived her spirits immensely.

By chance Major Benjy and Heather Gillespie were passing as Miss Mapp made her theatrical dash (in reality more of a sedate rolling trot) down the road, her coat buttoned carefully askew and her hat perched on her head back to front.

'So sorry! Can't stop!' she trilled as she sped past. However, her degree of attention to her errand of urgency did not prevent her from wondering just where Major Flint and Mrs Gillespie had been that they were now heading homewards at lunchtime, no shopping basket to be seen.

The landlord of the King's Arms could have enlightened her, since the Major and Heather Gillespie had spent the last hour or so in his saloon bar, the Major with three or four chota pegs and his companion with two large schooners of sherry, ensconced on a leather sofa in deep conversation. Every so often the Major would erupt into a lusty laugh and Heather would giggle quietly, touch him on the sleeve and look around anxiously to see whether they were being observed. In fact they were not. Tilling was not short of public houses, and though they were in the snug for a full hour, not a single other living soul put a head around the door for the duration of their stay.

They entered Major Benjy's house at about the same time that Miss Mapp finally put in her last-minute appearance at the church hall, clutching something large wrapped up in wax paper.

'Oh dear! Oh dear! I do hope I'm not too late!' she gasped.

'No indeed, Miss Mapp,' replied Evie Bartlett, who was waiting outside the door. 'Fortunately for you Mr Wyse has been delayed. I can't think what's happened to him. He's usually so punctual.'

'In that case,' beamed Miss Mapp, 'I'll just slip in and put this on the table.'

She went into the hall and closed the door carefully behind her. Unwrapping as she went, she approached the table. She placed her iced wreck on the table alongside the dozen or so contributions that were already upon it. She noticed with a sudden stab of rage that Diva had after all chosen to produce a chocolate cake, which looked stunning as it nestled under its dusting of icing sugar. How typical of Diva to be so devious! She had obviously surmised that Miss Mapp might attempt to steal her thunder, but also that she would have expected her stratagem to be suspected, hence this outrageous double bluff of doing exactly what it was that she was supposed to have done in the first place.

Miss Mapp breathed deeply and then turned away as she heard Mr Wyse's voice outside the door.

'So sorry, my dear Mrs Bartlett,' he was saying. 'Would you believe it, my chauffeur couldn't get the car started and so, by the time I had waited to see if he could manage it and then decided to walk after all, I fear that I must have wasted ten minutes or so.'

It was at this moment that Elizabeth Mapp was seized by one of those moments of sheer inspiration that strike only once or twice during the average lifetime. Without even really thinking about what she was doing she turned back to the table, took the flag out of Diva's cake, stuck it into the icing on her own, picked up the one remaining paper flag, which had 'Miss Mapp' written upon it, and stuck it carefully in the existing little hole on the chocolate cake. There! That would show that nasty, underhand Diva Plaistow!

Mr Wyse opened the door, and looked most surprised to see anyone there.

'Dear Mr Wyse, do come in,' said Miss Mapp. 'I was just leaving. I was so late, I'm afraid, that I was only just in time to slip my poor little effort amongst all the others, ready for the august attention of the judge.'

She gave a mock curtsey, swaying perilously on the way up.

'Now I shall leave you to your judging.'

Mr Wyse opened the door for her, bowed, and then closed the door again and wandered over to the cake table to begin his deliberations.

There was one cake which stood out because it was such an awful mess. At first he assumed that it was something which a young girl had produced in her cookery class at school, but even making due allowance for want of aptitude and experience it was an appalling sight. It brought to mind a snowman which had been but crudely crafted in the first place, and then allowed to half-melt overnight. He put on his glasses and drew in his breath sharply as he made out the name on the flag. How on earth was it possible that Mrs Plaistow, of all people, the very same Mrs Plaistow who had occasionally spoken of displaying her baking talents for professional purposes, could possibly have produced something like this?

Mr Wyse was not proficient at the *Times* crossword for nothing, and his intellect whirred into overdrive. Eliminate what was impossible and whatever was left, no matter how improbable, must be the truth. (He was also a fan of Sherlock Holmes.) Clearly Diva could not have intended to submit a monstrosity like this. Therefore she must have felt forced to do so. Come to think of it, for all the wonderful cakes of hers which he had sampled over the years, he could not remember one which had been iced. Perhaps she had decided to branch into pastures new, and had realised too late that icing was a skill all of its own which she would have done well to master before attempting it for public gaze. Yes, that must be it. Mr Wyse shook his head sadly and decided chivalrously that the best thing to do with this particular entry was to ignore it altogether.

As his gaze wandered to and fro over the table, his eyes were drawn again and again to a succulent-looking chocolate cake dusted with icing sugar. Mr Wyse had a particularly weak spot for chocolate cake, and this one seemed quite superb. As he bent closer, the welcoming aroma of chocolate seemed to beckon him ever closer. So close, in fact, that the name on its flag suddenly leapt into prominence and he drew back with a sigh of dismay. It was impossible, of course, after the events of yesterday, that Miss Mapp should be awarded the prize. He imagined himself having to inform his sister Amelia that he had disregarded her comments of the previous day; it was but a brief imagining. There had been a distressing scene during his childhood when he had refused to allow Amelia to play with his favourite spinning top; the physical scars had eventually healed, but he had been unable to look at fire tongs without an involuntary shudder ever since. No, he had no wish to tweak the dragon's tail when it might safely be left undisturbed.

Since the chocolate cake was out of the question, the selection process was soon narrowed down to two fruitcakes, both of which appeared equally worthy of his favour. However, on closer inspection one of them had been entered by Evie Bartlett and the other by somebody of whom Mr Wyse had never heard, so with due solemnity he took a small blue rosette out of his jacket pocket and placed it on the ecclesiastical candidate.

He opened the door, where Evie was still waiting.

'All done, Mrs Bartlett,' he said with a little bow, 'and may I be the first to congratulate you. Quite the most delicious fruitcake I have seen for a long time.'

Evie squeaked excitedly and locked the door behind them.

'Now, Mr Wyse, we must both remember to be back a little before two to welcome the Mayor.'

'I shall be there,' said Mr Wyse with the air of a man who is conscious of being chided for having just arrived late, 'you may rely upon it.'

Miss Mapp had in the meantime been putting into execution the second part of her plan. Proceeding at a more normal ambulatory pace, she had retraced her steps the short distance from the church hall to Mallards, and then carried on to the Major's house, where she knocked on the door. This brought forth no immediate response, which puzzled her as she was sure that the Major and Mrs Gillespie had been heading homewards when she last saw them. So she knocked again, but still without any noticeable response. Then, just as she was turning to leave with a look of intense vexation on her face, the Major's bedroom window opened overhead and he looked out. Miss Mapp could not help but notice that he did not appear to be wearing a collar and tie.

'What is it?' he enquired curtly and then, seeing Miss Mapp, his tone changed to one of surprise.

'Ah, Miss Elizabeth,' he said.

'As if his neighbour was the most unlikely person in the whole world to be knocking on his door in the middle of the day,' thought Miss Mapp to herself crossly.

'Dear Major Benjy,' she cooed, 'I have come to ask the weeniest favour from you. I do hope you don't mind.'

'Ah, no, of course not,' he replied. A slight pause then ensued, after which Miss Mapp enquired, as tactfully as possible, whether it might not be better to continue the discussion in the Major's living room.

'Of course, of course,' cried the Major as if he had just been thinking the same thing himself, 'but you must excuse me for a few minutes. I'm afraid that I am not properly attired to receive a lady. I was just having a little lie-down, you know.'

'That's quite all right, Major,' Miss Mapp responded, though she was hoping that this doorstep conversation would come to an end as soon as possible, since she was already starting to get a crick in her neck from craning her head backwards so awkwardly. 'You take as much time as you need.'

The window closed again as abruptly as it had been opened, and as it did so it was almost as if a man's voice, sounding very much like the Major's, had said, 'The damn woman wants to come in.' But as, of course, that could not be so, Miss Mapp told herself, it must have been merely a trick of the wind. She could not help but wonder why it was that the Gillespie woman was apparently incapable of answering the door as might be expected of her. Perhaps it was her afternoon off? But no, she had seen her only twenty minutes ago walking home with the Major. Here was another mystery, then.

After a minute or two the Major could be heard descending the stairs rather heavily. He opened the door to Miss Mapp, clad in what had once obviously been a rather splendid Chinese silk dressing gown but which was now somewhat faded and starting to look as threadbare as the tiger-skin rug which the Major claimed variously to have killed with a Mauser rifle in Bengal, with an elephant gun in Rajasthan and with the single sword stroke, on that famous day in the Punjab, which saved the life of a maharajah, no less, in the process. Indeed, Miss Mapp had been heard to venture that if she had been killed as many times as Major Flint's tiger, then doubtless she would be looking a little the worse for wear herself.

She noted with some relief that the Major was at least respectably clad on this occasion so far as nether garments were concerned. However, he was wearing carpet slippers instead of shoes and socks.

'Please excuse my dress,' he said, catching her glance. 'I was having a lie-down, as I said, and I thought you wouldn't mind a little informality between friends.'

'Of course not, dear Major,' she replied, 'though I am a little surprised that Gillespie could not open the door to me.'

'Ah!' said the Major. Miss Mapp waited a moment or two, but it became clear that this was all the reply which the Major was intending to provide.

'She is well, I trust?' she continued.

'Ah!' said the Major again. However, this time Miss Mapp simply raised her eyebrows quizzically and gazed at him, thus making it clear to even the meanest intelligence, she thought, that some substantive response was expected to be forthcoming.

'No, actually, not at all well, I don't think. Matter of fact, I believe she's having a little lie-down herself. Women's problems, I shouldn't wonder,' he concluded, hoping that Miss Mapp would not be so indelicate as to enquire further.

'Really? You surprise me,' she persisted, clearly unabashed by any possibility of indelicacy. 'She looked quite well when I saw you together a little while ago.'

'Yes, yes indeed,' countered the Major, 'curious thing, that; most curious. No sooner had we got in than the woman complained of feeling unwell and went to bed. Haven't had sight nor sound of her since.'

He stroked his moustache in what seemed a very concerned way. As he did so, there came what sounded remarkably like the noises of somebody moving around upstairs.

'Well,' said Miss Mapp, 'let us hope that she makes a speedy recovery. In fact,' she continued as there came the definite sound of a door opening and closing and footsteps passing along the upstairs landing, 'it seems that we may congratulate her upon it already.'

The Major fancied that the conversation was beginning to fasten unnecessarily on Mrs Gillespie's state of health, and decided to change the subject.

'Forgive me, Miss Elizabeth,' he said, 'but you did say that you had a favour to ask of me.'

'And so I do,' she replied. She fixed him with her beadiest of stares. 'However, before I do so, I must impress upon you the need for the utmost secrecy, though I fear I cannot reveal the circumstances which prompt what may seem a rather odd request.'

'I hope, dear Miss Elizabeth,' the Major said with a manly glint in his eye, 'that no lady in need, least of all a particular friend such as yourself, will ever find Major Benjamin Flint wanting in such matters.'

'I have no doubt of that, dear Major Benjy,' she said girlishly. Suddenly she felt slightly short of breath. Really, how magnificent the Major could be when he chose! She could not conceive of anyone she would rather have by her side in a moment of crisis. Very well, let her give her knight his quest, and then be off home to take the emery board to her corns.

'As I say, this may seem a rather strange request, but I would like you to be at the church hall when the Spring Show opens at two, or even better at a little before two, and buy my cake for me. I am sure dear Mr Wyse will have removed the names from each cake after judging, to avoid any unneighbourly comparisons. So thoughtful, of course. But you will be able to recognise it, as it is the only one covered in icing.'

The major gaped at her with a sad lack of comprehension.

'But, Miss Elizabeth, why on earth would you want to buy your own cake?' he enquired.

'Dear Major, I did tell you that I could not divulge the circumstances,' she said severely.

'Quite! Quite!' he acknowledged. 'I am duly rebuked, but fear not, dear lady, your wish is my command. I will do your bidding. Your cake shall indeed be bought by yours truly as soon as the show opens.'

Miss Mapp was greatly relieved to hear that her interests would be so well protected, and rose to leave for home. However, there was one matter which was still puzzling her and she broached it directly, with scant regard for the Major's generous pledge of support.

'I didn't know that it was your custom to indulge in a siesta, Major,' she said.

'Ah!' said the Major. 'Yes, indeed. Acquired the habit in India, don't you know. In fact, I was just telling Mrs Gillespie about it earlier. Called a bhat-ghum out there, don't you know. Traditionally you get your babu to massage you with mustard oil first. Not sure why it has to be mustard, actually. I find any old oil will do. Bucks you up no end, Miss Elizabeth, you should try it.'

He became aware that Miss Mapp was staring at him rather coldly.

'Without the oil, perhaps?' he suggested. 'Yes, definitely, best thing. Not obligatory at all, you know, not at all.'

For once, Miss Mapp found herself wishing that she had refrained from making an impertinent enquiry about a neighbour's personal habits. She bade him farewell with what she trusted was the right juxtaposition of maidenly gratitude for a gentleman who was about to champion her cause, and cool reserve for one who had dared to think of oil being rubbed into her body. However, the latter thought made her suddenly feel somewhat flushed, and as she hobbled the short distance back to Mallards (for in truth her corns were hurting her rather badly) she feared that this may well have undermined the effect which she had been seeking to convey.

Time had been passing the while, and the Major only just had time to put on collar, tie, socks and shoes before slipping on his second-best tweed jacket and making good his commitment to his visiting podiatric sufferer. He arrived at the hall promptly just before two and saw that the cake table was currently completely unattended except by a lady volunteer with a biscuit tin full of change and a pile of miscellaneous paper bags. He cast an eye over the exhibits and gave a gasp of horror at the sight of an iced monstrosity in the middle of the table.

He studied it close-up and then gave another gasp of horror as he saw the name 'Mrs Plaistow' written on a flag, which was stuck into the top of it. How on earth could Godiva Plaistow have produced such a ham-fisted effort? Here was a mystery indeed. Ah, yes! Here was Elizabeth Mapp's cake with her name on it, covered in icing sugar as she had said. He could only assume, as he admired both the appearance and the smell of this stunning example of the cake-maker's art, that she had so fallen in love with her creation that she could not bear anyone to enjoy it but herself and, he earnestly hoped, himself. He was particularly partial to chocolate cake, and this one looked an absolute beauty. In fact, he could not understand why it had not won the prize, for that honour had clearly fallen to Evie Bartlett, as signified by the blue rosette crowning her own effort. Damned unfair, in his view.

Some dozen or so people had now filed into the hall and Mr Wyse obviously felt that this constituted enough of a quorum to rap delicately on a table with the end of his cane for silence, and introduce the Mayor, whom he invited to open the proceedings with a few words. While his worship was doing so, the Major saw Lucy enter the hall and head in his direction. He noted with approval that she was wearing a pair of riding jodhpurs which did little to hide the magnificent curves of her figure.

With an exactitude of timing she had surely never intended (she had in fact feared she was going to be late), Lucy reached the cake stand just as the Mayor drew to a close his thanks to the organisers, and declared the proceedings open.

'Good afternoon,' said the Major politely, raising his cap.

'Good afternoon to you, Major,' replied Lucy cheerfully. Remarkably, the inconvenient fact that she had but recently struck him hard on the head with his own stick seemed to have been completely forgotten.

'Been riding, I see?' queried the Major, thinking this was really rather a clever thing to come up with on the spur of the moment.

'Nothing gets past you, I see,' said Lucy. 'Don't tell me the jodhpurs gave it away?'

'If you'll excuse me,' said the Major rather stiffly, 'I have an errand to perform.' He turned away and made his purchase.

'So have I, as it happens,' said Lucy. 'Now, let me see – good God!' She gazed at the iced monstrosity in consternation.

'Indeed.' The Major shook his head sorrowfully. 'A sad lapse by one of our neighbours, what? Best say nothing, I think.'

He raised his hat again and strolled away, carefully bearing his purchase before him. Lucy, who in studying the table for herself had not seen which cake he had bought, could only stare in mounting horror and incomprehension at the cake which clearly had Diva's name on it for all to see. No wonder that poor Diva had wanted her to buy it as soon as the show opened! She must have been absolutely devastated when her efforts had gone so horribly awry, and desperate that nobody should see it if at all possible. She probably reckoned that Mr Wyse could be relied upon to keep mum, after all he was famous for his tact and discretion, and had hoped that Lucy would get there before anybody else. At this thought, a wave of guilt flooded through her. If only she had been there before the show opened she would have left the money on the table, taken the cake and be damned to the proprieties. As it was, Major Benjy had seen it, and would surely pass the news on to Miss Mapp, despite his suggestion that nothing should be said. Poor Diva!

With a heavy heart she paid for her purchase, took it home and threw it away in the dustbin, still wrapped in the paper bag which the cake table had provided. Then she ran herself a hot bath, stripped off her riding clothes and treated herself to a jolly good soak, a glass of gin and French resting ready to hand on the floor beside her, and tried to work out how best to break the news to Diva that she had failed her.

Chapter 7

The next day being Sunday, Lucy was able to waylay Diva on her way to church. This plan necessitated a change from her normal habits, since she and Irene were irregular worshippers at best, but the importance of her mission overcame the urge to lounge in bed with a pot of tea and the weekend papers, which is how they usually passed a Sunday morning until Irene became bored and started drawing irreverent cartoons of both national politicians and local residents in the newspaper margins, sometimes hopelessly commingled in such a way that a particularly pugnacious Winston Churchill was being beaten into submission with an umbrella by a hag-like Miss Mapp.

So it was that Lucy was hovering nervously on the corner of the High Street outside the King's Arms as Diva opened her front door and stepped out. To add to Lucy's burden of guilt still further she smiled brightly and said, 'Hello, Lucy, I can't tell you how grateful I am for your help yesterday. Here's the half a crown, by the way.'

'Oh, that's all right,' said Lucy awkwardly, slipping the coin into her jacket pocket. 'I say, Diva, something awful happened. Major Benjy was there when the show opened as well, and I'm rather afraid he saw your cake.'

'Well, that's all right, dear,' said Diva soothingly, 'since you bought it and threw it away nobody will ever cut into it, so there's no harm done, is there?'

'Decent of you to take it that way, Diva,' said Lucy, much relieved. 'I must say that it was jolly brave of you to put it in at all. If it had been me, I wouldn't have wanted anyone seeing it.'

'Oh, I don't think it looked as bad as all that, did it?' asked Diva vaguely. 'Do excuse me, Lucy, there's Evie Bartlett, and I haven't had a chance to offer my congratulations.'

Diva hurried across the road to greet the conquering heroine of the Tilling baking competition. Evie, who was on her own as the Padre was already robing himself in the vestry, modestly accepted the praise that was due to her.

Conversation turned to their planned activities for the rest of the day.

'I say!' squeaked Evie suddenly. 'One of Kenneth's old seminary friends is coming in his motor car to take us into Brighton this afternoon. Why don't you come with us? He's a single gentleman, and I'm sure there will be room in the car.'

Diva was not one to turn down an afternoon in Brighton and probably, though she was not quite sure, a single gentleman either. Whatever the case, it sounded an inviting prospect and she and Evie walked off to church together, chattering happily. Diva felt a momentary twinge of embarrassment as she passed the Wyses getting out of their Rolls Royce, but Mr Wyse simply raised his hat and said 'Charmed, ladies,' with a very pleasant smile.

Miss Mapp was walking along some distance behind Diva, and the Wyses had exited the car and were falling in on the pavement when she arrived. Mr Wyse raised his hat again, though the 'Good mornings' from the various female branches of the Wyse clan were at best perfunctory.

'Dear Mr Wyse,' said Miss Mapp, fixing him with the bright smile of one eager for information, 'urbane crossword expert that you are, I wonder if you could assist poor little me with a definition?'

'If I can, certainly, dear lady,' replied the urbane Mr Wyse urbanely.

'Well, Major Benjy has been telling me about how back in India he used to get a baboon to rub him down with mustard oil, and I know that can't be right. Can't baboons be terribly dangerous?'

Mr Wyse concurred that they could indeed be very dangerous if crossed – rather like sisters, he added to himself.

'Are you sure he said "baboon", Miss Mapp? Perhaps it was just a word that sounded like "baboon". But, if so, what could it be, I wonder? Not "balloon", certainly. That wouldn't make sense at all.'

'No, quite,' said Miss Mapp.

'From the context, it sounds as though it must be a person,' mused Mr Wyse. 'Hmm, let me see, a Hindu word perhaps? We have lots of those, you know, "tiffin", "khaki", "pukkah", for example. Oh yes indeed, lots and lots of Indian words have entered everyday English usage.'

He smiled contemplatively at this thought, but Miss Mapp could not help but think that he was straying from the point, nor could she help but bring this to his attention.

'Quite right, quite right, madam,' he said with a little bow. 'Now, come along, Algernon,' he reproved himself firmly, 'this can't really be all that difficult. A Hindu word for a person with army connections which sounds like "baboon". Hmm … ah!'

This was not like one of Major Flint's 'Ah's, which tended to be loud, hearty, confident and ultimately meaningless. Mr Wyse's 'Ah' was the unmistakeable distress call of the greater plumed East Sussex gentleman who realises that he is in possession of information which has been requested by a lady, but which it is quite impossible to convey to her with the least modicum of decorum.

'Dear Miss Mapp,' he said with obvious agitation, 'I find myself in a delicate, perhaps even an embarrassing position. Were I to give you the information which you request, which of course I yearn to do' – he paused and bowed gravely in her direction – 'it might, I fear, place the Major in an unfavourable light. Not,' he added hastily, 'that there might not be some perfectly innocent explanation.'

'Dear Mr Wyse,' responded Miss Mapp in kind, 'how very like you to show such sensitivity. However' – at this point she paused and smiled, succeeding only in baring her teeth, which Mr Wyse found most alarming – 'unless it is of course quite impossible, I would very much appreciate the answer to my question.'

Mr Wyse, images of teeth and fire tongs blurring together in his mind, felt his resolve weaken. He struggled to find words to soften the impact of his news.

'I understand that out in India the young officers take a female servant to look after them. Fulfil all the domestic offices, in fact.'

'Dear Mr Wyse, how kind of you to be so sensitive, but you need not have worried. I see nothing improper in a little washing and cleaning.'

Had Mr Wyse been any normal man he would have left matters there, raised his hat and accompanied Miss Mapp into church. Unfortunately Mr Wyse was not a normal man, but a pedant. A charming pedant, certainly, but a pedant nonetheless. Without a thought for the consequences he felt impelled to clarify the full meaning of the word.

'Oh no, Miss Mapp, I see you have not fully grasped my meaning. When I say "all the domestic offices", I mean everything which a wife could provide. The babu lives with her officer, I understand, exactly as if …'

'Yes, thank you, Mr Wyse,' Miss Mapp cut in quickly. 'I find my curiosity is quite satisfied, thank you.'

Now Mr Wyse did raise his hat and ask Miss Mapp if he could accompany her into church, just a few moments later than he should have done. Miss Mapp, however, felt her emotions to be in such turmoil that she asked to be excused and milled rather aimlessly around in the church square for a few minutes. Finally she realised that she was in danger of missing the start of the service and walked determinedly towards the door. As she did so, other latecomers put in an appearance. It was Mr and Mrs Twemlow, who ran the grocer's shop just around the corner.

'Good morning, Miss Mapp,' they chorused respectfully.

'Good morning,' replied Miss Mapp absently, her thoughts engaged elsewhere. 'Tell me,' she said suddenly, her speech following those very thoughts, 'was that Mrs Gillespie I saw in the shop yesterday afternoon?'

'Yes indeed, mum,' replied Mrs Twemlow. 'Asking for mustard oil, if you please. I said I didn't know what it was, and that we didn't stock it any old how. Mustard oil indeed! Lord knows what she wanted it for.'

The church service passed entirely without incident, save only that one of the choirboys was discovered to be trying to set fire to a hassock with a magnifying glass and the help of the early summer sun streaming through the Burne-Jones stained-glass window. The Padre's sermon on the text 'If we say that we have no sin we deceive ourselves, and the truth is not in us' was workmanlike rather than inspiring, though everyone tried very hard to look as unsinful and undeceitful as possible, while wondering at which individual in the congregation the Padre was aiming his blandishments; there had been rumours lately about Mrs Twistevant being seen in the bushes near the old harbour with the man who delivered their potatoes, though she had dismissed the episode, when questioned by her husband, as nothing more sensational than brambling for blackberries.

Looking around the church, it was obvious to all that the Major was not present. This was most unusual. Like the true military man that he was, he was extremely regular in his habits, and church parade, as he invariably referred to it, was a staple of his week. He would sing the hymns loudly and melodiously, snore gently during the sermon and salute the Padre solemnly afterwards, before dismissing himself from parade and strolling to one of Tilling's numerous public houses to reflect with due but transient sobriety on the Sabbath morning experience. Though perhaps not spiritually uplifted during communion, he was frequently so by the time that

Sunday licensing hours sent him back into the light of day in search of his lunch.

His absence was naturally a matter of some conjecture during the spontaneous conversations which always arose outside church. Perhaps he was ill? Perhaps he was travelling and was planning on making his devotions at a church elsewhere? Nobody knew, though everyone was happy to venture a suggestion. Within a few minutes one story had spread that he had suffered a recurrence of his bilharzia (Lucy, now joined by Quaint Irene), another that he had simply overslept (Diva and the Wyse clan), and yet another that he had suddenly been called away to Windsor Castle to attend upon the maharajah whose life he had saved and be introduced to the King (Miss Mapp).

Discussion was brought to a close by the arrival of a dilapidated old Hillman, which parked rather apologetically beside the Wyses' Rolls Royce and disgorged a middle-aged clergyman who could happily have modelled for the 'before' photograph of a 'before and after' advertisement for a firm of ecclesiastical outfitters. From a distance, he appeared to have a yellowish muffler tied around the lower part of his face, but as he walked towards the church closer inspection revealed this to be nothing more than a set of very prominent teeth. Evie Bartlett seized upon him eagerly and introduced him to Diva as the Reverend Theophilus Oates.

The Reverend Oates was delighted, charmed and positively enraptured by the thought of Mrs Plaistow accompanying them to Brighton and absolutely insisted that she should do so, and that she should call him 'Theo' into the bargain, as Evie Bartlett already did. They were joined by the Padre, who had by now disrobed, and slipped away as quietly as possible in the circumstances, the Hillman having backfired massively as Mr Oates reversed and sent every gull in Tilling into flight, wheeling and cawing around the town.

Diva was determined to enjoy her drive through the Sussex countryside, as a ride in a motor car was for her a very rare experience.

However, she could not help but notice a very strong smell of general mustiness, most of which seemed to emanate from the Reverend Oates himself. He had insisted that she sit in the front with him, and she was thus well placed to observe at first hand the alarm on the face of a cyclist as he swerved on to the Belvedere platform to avoid the oncoming Hillman and performed an elegant somersault over the handlebars of his bicycle. Mr Oates seemed not to notice this, or if he did he was not fazed by it, and pressed on heartily, though he was apparently a motorist of free-spirited views who paid scant regard to such outdated concepts as driving on the left, or to petty regulations which he might find too restrictive, such as traffic signals or speed limits. From the back seat, Evie gave a little scream, hastily stifled, as they approached the Landgate in fine style, and somehow managed to negotiate it without loss of life.

As they headed out of Tilling Mr Oates suddenly said, 'Here's a good one for you, Kenneth. Have you heard the story about the parishioner whose bicycle gets stolen, and he asks his vicar to help him find it?'

'I dinnae think so,' said the Padre cautiously.

'Well, here's the thing you see. The vicar tells Old Bob, that's his name, you know, tells Old Bob not to worry. He says he'll preach a sermon on the ten commandments and when he gets to "Thou shall not steal" he will stop and gaze meaningfully around the church and ten bob to a tanner if the reprobate doesn't have an attack of guilt and leave Old Bob's bike outside his house that very night.' He broke off to grin over his shoulder at the Bartletts in the back seat, a move which caused the car to swerve alarmingly on to the wrong side of the road. The Padre flinched and then tried to pretend that he hadn't.

'Well, sure enough, the next day Old Bob comes to see the vicar and thanks him for his help in getting his bike back. "There you are, Bob," says the vicar, "I told you what would happen when I got to 'Thou shall not steal'." "Oh no, sir," cries Bob. "It was when you got to 'Thou shall not commit adultery' that I remembered where I'd left it."'

Sitting in the front seat and staring straight ahead, it was impossible for Diva to observe the Bartletts' demeanour, so she decided to play safe and pretend not to understand. She heard a little gasp from Evie and then the Padre said, 'Steady on, Theo,' without any trace of a Scottish accent.

Meanwhile, Diva became aware of a very strange and rather worrying sound, like a rusty saw being drawn through wood repeatedly, with quickening speed, and accompanied by gasping noises. Clearly something was very wrong with the car. She had no idea of the technical issues involved, but imagined that either a wheel was about to fall off or the engine was about to explode. Then she realised that this was actually the sound of the Reverend Oates laughing. She realised at about the same moment that either in order to provide some sort of safety valve for his mirth, or simply to show appreciation for the story, his left hand was slapping a thigh vigorously. Her thigh.

This was a wholly new experience for Godiva Plaistow, and she felt herself beginning to panic. Was she supposed to enjoy this experience? It was in fact not entirely unpleasant, apart from the fact that in his exuberance he was slapping her rather hard and probably raising a bruise. If so, was she supposed to express her enjoyment in some way, either by smiling indulgently or (surely not?) slapping his own thigh in return? Or was she, on the contrary, supposed to react with outraged horror and order him to stop the car and drive her home? She decided that the safest thing to do was to savour the experience for a little longer before deciding.

She was just on the point of making up her mind that perhaps to say 'Not so hard, please, Theo' might strike the right note of compromise, when the Reverend Oates attempted simultaneously to slap her thigh, change gear and negotiate a hairpin bend. Since these activities would have required the combined resources of at least three hands and he had only two, it was inevitable that he would fail to complete at least one of these tasks. Giving it up as a bad job, he abandoned all attempts at turning the corner and allowed the Hillman to run straight on into a field, narrowly missing an oncoming charabanc in the process, and bumping alarmingly over the ruts.

This time both Diva and Evie screamed out loud. So, to his shame, did the Padre.

Entirely unabashed, Mr Oates brought the car to a halt, said, 'Sorry about that, everyone, I've been meaning to have those brakes looked at,' beamed at the white-faced occupants of the back seat and reversed rather abruptly back on to the road.

The remainder of the journey passed relatively without incident, save only that Mr Oates at one point launched into what promised to be an amusing but entirely unsuitable narrative about a verger and a lady parishioner, whereupon both the Bartletts started talking very loudly about their labrador being off her food.

They drove right down to the sea and parked on Madeira Drive. Mr Oates pulled a watch from his pocket and suggested that they should go in search of a rather jolly little beach restaurant he remembered from his last visit, but Diva was intrigued by some small train tracks running alongside the road.

'What on earth are those?' she asked. 'They look like the tram tracks in Tilling that take Major Flint off to the links every day.'

'That, dear lady,' boomed the Reverend Oates, 'is Volk's electric railway, and I positively insist that we all travel upon it forthwith. It's tremendous fun, and quite harmless.' This last phrase was added quickly as Diva, the memory of the journey still fresh in her mind, looked momentarily uncomfortable at the thought of using anything other than her own feet for the purposes of locomotion.

They strolled towards the pier and the starting point of the railway line. Mr Oates proved unexpectedly knowledgeable on such an arcane subject, and explained that it had been the first truly electric railway in Britain.

'What about the London Underground?' ventured Evie Bartlett.

'Why bless you, Evie, that was steam until quite recently. This has been here since about 1880, I believe, and ...'

'I say!' exclaimed Diva suddenly. 'Why, surely that's Major Flint?'

'So then,' said Diva, 'once we realised it was that McGillicuddy woman, or whatever she's called, we followed them. Just to see what happened, of course.'

'Well now, Mistress Plaistow,' demurred the Padre, I would'nae say we followed them exactly. More that we simply happened to be going in the same direction at the same time.'

'That's right,' said Diva, unabashed. 'We just went in the same direction – to see what happened.'

'Diva, dear, really,' chided Miss Mapp.

'No, actually it's true,' protested Diva, realising to her surprise that it was indeed so. 'We had already decided to go on the electric railway and we just carried on with what we were going to do anyway.'

'Indeed, indeed, that was the way of it,' concurred the Padre, his conscience clearly considerably salved.

'I think I see what you're saying,' cooed Miss Mapp, which was her usual and widely acknowledged euphemism for accusing her neighbours, old and dear friends though they were, of lying through their teeth. 'You just happened to be going in the same direction at the same, and by pure chance slightly behind them, of course. Dear me, how convenient.'

'Come off it, Elizabeth,' said Diva stoutly. 'You know jolly well that you would have done exactly the same.'

'I'm sure I would not, Diva,' said Miss Mapp, with the air of one rising above a sordid squabble, 'but then I have always been noted for respecting the privacy of others.'

There was silence at this, as well there might be. Even the Padre found himself thinking distinctly uncharitable thoughts, since of course Miss Mapp was well known for exactly the opposite of the quality she had just claimed. He set himself to an inward recitation of 1 Corinthians 13, reflecting on the nature of charity.

'Well, then, Elizabeth,' said Diva calmly, 'in that case we cannot possibly compromise your integrity by telling you what we observed. Sorry to have mentioned it. Talk about something else, shall we? Much better, really.'

She sat back and sipped her tea demurely. Evie Bartlett squeaked delightedly. This was surely a masterstroke on Diva's part. Miss Mapp wanted to know more, and everyone knew she wanted to know more, much more. Now she would have to ask. In fact, if Diva had anything to do with it, she would have to beg.

'So, Padre, how much money did we raise from the Spring Show this year?' enquired Diva.

'Well, Mistress Plaistow, I have a fancy that it will be a wee thing more than thirty pounds,' replied the Padre gravely, though secretly he was enjoying himself very much indeed. It seemed a mean thing to inform on a man, though the two lady members of the party did not seem to see it that way, but being able to witness Miss Mapp's temporary discomfiture made it feel at least partially worthwhile. The words of the *Book of Common Prayer* came to him as if wafted over the ether: 'Create in me a clean heart, O God, and renew a right spirit within me.'

'Thirty pounds!' marvelled Diva. 'Why, Elizabeth, did you ever think that it would be so much?'

'No, indeed, Diva dear, everyone has excelled themselves this year,' beamed Miss Mapp. She resolved that she must somehow teach Diva Plaistow a terrible lesson for this impossible position in which she had placed her. Everyone knew that she had a legitimate interest in hearing about Major Benjy, and had simply been displaying the natural reluctance that any civilised person would have shown, and that any civilised neighbour would have instantly recognised and accepted, she concluded. After all, it was well known that she and the Major enjoyed a certain understanding, though the precise nature of this understanding had never fully been grasped by him, despite her gentle yet persistent prompting.

It really was quite intolerable that she was now going to have to affect a crude prurience which was so much at odds with her natural character, and which could not fail to show her in a bad light with the Bartletts, as Diva was well aware. She became aware that Diva had just asked her another question, and suddenly inspiration struck.

'I'm so sorry, Diva dear,' she said. 'Did you ask me something? I didn't notice. Rude of me, I know.'

The Bartletts glanced at each other and then buried their faces in their tea cups. This was truly a masterly display of insouciance by Miss Mapp, and they intended to relish every second of it.

'Thinking of something else, perhaps?' asked Diva. 'Or someone else, more like,' she added archly.

'Diva, dear,' came Miss Mapp's rejoinder, her smile broader and sweeter than ever, 'You are correct as always. I was just thinking that you must all come to tea with me tomorrow – properly to tea, I mean. The truth is that I was very naughty and took a little peek at that chocolate cake recipe which you were studying so avidly in the library. Shall I confess? Very well! I have attempted it, Diva, and while I am sure that my efforts will not be as magnificent as your own I would very much like you all to try it.'

She could not but rejoice that circumstances had fallen so neatly into place. She had been greatly puzzled, not to mention exasperated, when the Major had brought the wrong cake to Mallards. She had thought her instructions explicit enough for even a man to understand and follow. Then, when she realised the tiny name flag was still stuck into it, she realised that the Major had, on the contrary, rendered her an enormous service. She had felt sure that Mr Wyse would remove all the name flags after he had finished judging, thus rendering the cakes anonymous, but clearly this had not happened for some reason. Perhaps he had been in a hurry to get home for his lunch, or had simply forgotten. Whatever the reason, Major Benjy had saved her stratagem from discovery and public exposure, and she was deeply grateful: not that she intended to let him see that, of course.

She had then experienced a stab of panic at the thought that if the name flag had been left in the chocolate cake, it would also have been left in the iced monstrosity. Donning her hat, she had dashed round to the church hall only to find that the cake was missing and, according to the lady running the stall, had been snapped up eagerly by Lucy in the opening moments of the show. Whatever Lucy could have wanted with such an object was beyond her, but whatever the case the crisis had passed and Miss Mapp was well and truly master of the situation. She had carefully placed the chocolate cake in a very well-sealed cake tin for later use, for already the seeds of an idea had been taking shape in her mind. Now the moment had arrived for these individual threads of ingenuity to coalesce into one defining act of genius. She would pass Diva's cake off as her own, nobody (not even Diva) would know that this was not the case, and everyone, including Diva, would have little option but to bestow fulsome but well-deserved praise upon it.

Miss Mapp's cup of happiness bubbled over inwardly, melting even her determination not to give in to Diva's silly little game. She knew that Diva was bursting to tell her news and that sooner or later she would be forced to do so. However, this might take some time and necessitate another pot of tea, and with Earl Grey currently at one and tuppence a pound in Twemlow's this was a valid consideration.

'Now come along, Diva,' she said briskly. 'Stop all this nonsense and tell us whatever it is that you are so eager for us all to know.'

Diva was momentarily speechless.

'Eager?' she gasped. 'If you remember, you were not at all eager to hear it. In fact, you told me not to tell you any more.'

'My, my, what a fuss you do make, Diva,' said Miss Mapp soothingly. 'Now, nonsense or not, just tell us your story and be done with it.'

'So you do want to know after all,' cried Diva triumphantly. 'Why, I count that as a moral victory to me, then.'

Miss Mapp felt her forbearance being sorely tried. She felt a very strong urge indeed to say 'Fiddlesticks', or something scathing preceded by 'Diva, dear, old friends though we are ...', but time was passing and she directed an anxious glance at the teapot.

'Moral victory if you say so, dear,' she replied, 'though I honestly haven't the slightest idea to what you are referring, I'm sure.'

Diva drew another sharp breath at this, and went rather red in the face with suppressed rage. Then she reminded herself that she was about to tell possibly the most scandalous story in the whole history of Tilling, and she forced herself to be calm.

'Well,' she said, 'they got off the little train at the end of the line – the end away from the pier, that is. They went into a little café and we followed them. I mean, we had already decided to go into that very café and just happened to be walking along behind them.'

'Why not call a spade a spade?' demanded Miss Mapp hotly. 'I would call that "following", plain and simple.' Then she remembered that Tilling's own Padre had been one of the shadowing party, and stopped. 'But do go on, of course.'

'Well, it all happened before they got to the café, actually. You see, we were sitting in the last carriage of the tram, or train, or whatever you call it, and we could see them up ahead of us in the first carriage. They had their heads very close together as though they were whispering to each other, and then she put up her parasol so we couldn't see them anymore.'

'Oh,' said Evie in her high-pitched voice, 'but we did see ...'

'Yes, yes, I'm coming to that,' interrupted Diva, fearful that Evie might steal her thunder.

'When they got off the train he got out first, of course, and helped her off. Then he offered her his arm, Elizabeth, and she took it.'

'No!' exclaimed Miss Mapp, for all the world as if they were exchanging news in the street, shopping baskets in hand.

'Yes!' responded Diva. 'And that's only the half of it, Elizabeth. You see, while they were walking away from the train, we saw him, from behind of course, we saw him move his hand away from her arm and ... well, touch her.'

'Touch her? Touched her where?' queried Miss Mapp. 'Or "touched her what", should that be?'

'Really, Elizabeth!' said Diva, deeply shocked.

'Surely it is an important part of your story?' asked Miss Mapp. 'So far, there is nothing you have said that places Major Flint in an ungentlemanly light. Misguided quite possibly, unwise, certainly, but nothing improper.'

'Then I must tell you, Elizabeth, and prepare yourself for a shock, that we saw him stroking – and in public, mind ...'

Her voice tailed off as she struggled to think of a way of expressing delicately something which she realised with increasing horror was quite impossible to phrase decently, especially with the Padre in the room.

'... a certain part of her anatomy,' she finished rather lamely.

'And what part of her anatomy would that be, exactly?' Miss Mapp asked. 'Her arm, I suppose?' she added, with just a hint of her trademark sarcasm, which normally closed a subject for good.

'No. Much worse. Much, much worse. And in public, too, Elizabeth,' tapped out Diva in her telegraphic style.

'Indeed?' said Mapp, or rather asked, the repeat of her earlier query being (she trusted) all too obvious even to dear Diva, who was frequently rather slow on the uptake. However, just to be on the safe side she arched her eyebrows in what she knew from frequent practice in front of the living-room mirror to be an effective inquisitorial manner.

As the enormity of having to answer the question registered fully on the assembled number, a long pause ensued. Diva stuffed a large piece of cake into her mouth. After all, she reasoned, nobody could be expected to answer any question with a mouth full of fruitcake.

Evie Bartlett squeaked repeatedly but indistinctly, while the Padre yodelled a series of Scottish-sounding vowels up and down a scale of about an octave and a half from which nothing much could be discerned except possibly 'Ye ken'. Finally, Diva could stand it no longer, and decided to put Elizabeth out of (or rather into) her misery.

'Posterior,' she said firmly, ejaculating a storm of fruitcake fragments equally firmly. 'No sense beating about the bush. He was touching her on her posterior. Two or three times just while we were watching ... I mean, while we just happened to see them, that is.'

Miss Mapp blanched and swayed in her chair. She thought briefly of essaying a rather effective fainting manoeuvre which she had been trying out in the privacy of her bedroom for some weeks now, which was designed to be carried out while standing, starting with a rather fetching crumpling at the knees and a despairing but somehow rather abstracted clutch for support at the nearest item of furniture. She decided against it, however, partly because she was not sure exactly how it might work out from a sitting position which afforded so little scope for a really good crumpling at the knees, and partly as the nearest item of furniture was a planter which supported a rather attractive flowerpot for which she had paid half a crown (daylight robbery though it had been) only a few days ago. This was all rather a shame, as she could have preceded it with a little cry of anguish which she kept for really special occasions, but she put such thoughts behind her, tempting though they were, and contented herself with leaning forward with a sharp intake of breath and pressing her thumb and forefinger tightly across the bridge of her nose as though to stem an incipient nosebleed.

'That poor woman,' she said, in a rather quavering voice which she hoped combined both a sense of her own deep horror (but at the same time, naturally, her own steadfast bravery in the face of such unpleasantness) and deep sisterly sympathy for a fellow female subjected to such indignities.

'Poor woman, nothing,' retorted Diva scornfully. Having successfully tacked her way out of a brief but perilous squall, she was now running free in fine form, the wind on her quarter and all guns run out for good measure.

'She was enjoying it. Slapped his hand and told him not to be naughty. Then the next time he did it she kissed him under her parasol. Thought nobody could see. Then they went in and had tea – Russian Caravan, I think,' she finished rather lamely, conscious that she may have placed the high drama of her narrative in peril by an unintended touch of bathos at its denouement.

She need not have worried. Horror, bravery and sisterly sympathy had vanished from Miss Mapp's mind and had been replaced with an emotion so precious, clean and intense that it is given to few mere mortals ever to be blessed by it. She felt herself irradiated with the sort of pure white light normally reserved for those in the grip of a deeply spiritual religious experience, and a beatific smile spread across her countenance. Her companions looked at each other uneasily, for they had seen that look before, and it did not bode well. As Miss Mapp lifted the teapot, they knew her to be flushed with self-knowledge, inner peace and a deep and burning desire for revenge.

Chapter 8

The next day Miss Mapp could be seen making an unaccustomed trip to the railway station. This was quite a long way away from the old town where she and her friends lived and she should probably have taken a taxi, but for the ruinous expense. However, by the time she reached the station she was beginning to regret this act of parsimony, understandable though it might be, as she was wearing her best day shoes and they were starting to hurt her feet quite dreadfully. She hoped that she might end up with a compartment to herself so that she could slip them off for a while.

She approached the booking office and bought a day return to Brighton. She glanced around her surreptitiously before adding, 'Second class, please.' She had already incurred the cost of two lengthy trunk calls the previous evening, and had no wish to commit yet another act of reckless extravagance quite so soon. She was also aware that the ticket collector had frequently finished his rounds by the time the Brighton train reached Tilling and so she might even risk sitting in a first-class compartment and brazening it out if he did in fact appear, claiming that she had requested a first-class ticket and that the stupid clerk in the booking office must have made a mistake. Major Benjy was reputed to have tried this himself the previous summer and to have given a stirring performance, marred only by his producing at the dramatic moment a platform ticket bought two weeks previously at Eastbourne. The threat of a summons to the magistrates' court had induced him to pay a hefty fine to the collector, after which he had stomped home in a fierce rage, drunk two large glasses of gin and had harsh words with his servant about gristle in his stewed mutton, at which she had burst into tears and given notice on the spot, costing him another half a crown the following morning in order to induce her to change her mind.

She considered buying a newspaper, but she already had one at home and saw no reason to waste threepence on another one. Instead she bought a magazine and settled herself in the ladies' waiting room. As there was nobody about, she surreptitiously eased her shoes off while she leafed through the magazine. It was difficult to concentrate, though, with thoughts of her delicious forthcoming revenge on Diva filling her mind, for it was that very afternoon when she was due to pass Diva's gorgeous chocolate cake off as the fruit of her own endeavours. Suddenly she heard the train whistle from the level crossing just outside town and regretted having taken her shoes off for such a short period of relief, particularly as her feet seemed to have swelled up slightly and she had great difficulty getting them on again. With one foot still not completely accommodated, she limped awkwardly on to the platform and into a first-class carriage, noticing as she did so that it was beginning to rain.

At about the same time as Miss Mapp was massaging her toes in a Southern Railway Pullman car, Lucy encountered an umbrella heading directly and almost horizontally towards her as she came round the corner into West Street from Porpoise Street. As she herself had her eyes screwed up against the driving rain which really had come up out of nowhere, she did not register this fact until the very last moment possible, which left her no time but to say 'Watch out!' very loudly and put the palms of both hands flat outwards before her, so that each pressed against a different panel of the oncoming threat. There was a sharp exclamation as the owner of the umbrella stumbled against the sudden resistance and then Lucy found herself in clumsy, half-staggering, half-dancing embrace with another woman. The upshot of all this was that the umbrella got dropped in the general confusion so that not only were both of them left staring at each rather stupidly, but each was simultaneously getting seriously and rapidly wet.

'I'm so sorry!' exclaimed Heather Gillespie, for she it was who had been driving an umbrella around the streets of Tilling without due care and attention. 'It came on to rain so suddenly that I came out without a raincoat, and I was hurrying to get home before I got soaked through. I do beg your pardon.'

'Don't worry,' said Lucy cheerfully. 'I say, I have the feeling that I've seen you around but I'm afraid I can't think of your name. Do excuse me.'

'I'm Heather Gillespie. I live just up the road; I'm looking after Major Flint. You're Lucy, I know, because he's pointed you out to me a couple of times.'

'Very pleased to meet you,' said Lucy formally, and then as she observed Heather's hair already plastered flat on her forehead the absurdity of their situation struck her.

'Here,' she said, opening the door of Taormina. 'Come in out of the rain until it stops.'

'You're very kind,' said Heather, 'but I really must get home. The Major will be back from golf any moment, and I must be there when he returns.'

'Nonsense,' said Lucy. 'I know Major Benjy's habits as if they were my own. First he'll spend a good half hour or so sheltering beside one the fairways and getting angrier and angrier, and then he'll make for the clubhouse. He'll be wet through by the time he reaches it, and he'll sit down in front of the fire to dry out and have a few chota pegs. Even if the rain stopped straightaway, which it's not going to, mind, even if it stopped straightaway he'd be at least an hour getting home.'

Heather hesitated, although she was conscious that she was getting wetter by the second.

'Oh, do come on!' cried Lucy impatiently. 'I'm getting soaked standing here.'

So it was that before she really knew what was happening Heather Gillespie found herself in the small front room of Taormina. She wasn't quite sure what to do with herself, as she did not want to make a chair wet by sitting on it, so she stood rather forlornly in the middle of the room, making a little puddle on the linoleum. Lucy came back into the room with two towels. One of these she threw at Heather, and with the other she started drying her hair furiously. Having had the benefit neither of umbrella nor raincoat, her summer dress clung to her like a second skin.

Taormina felt chilly and dark, and vaguely damp. As if to emphasise this point, the persistent drip, drip of water came from somewhere towards the back of the little house.

'God, I hate this place when it rains,' exclaimed Lucy. 'There's a hole in the roof which Irene can't afford to get fixed, and I'm sure there's rising damp, or falling damp or something, in the walls. Let's go in the other room, there's a stove in there.'

Heather followed Lucy into what was obviously used both as a studio and a general living area. There were half-finished canvases stacked against the wall, tubes of paint and brushes laid down and left any old how, and a faint smell of turpentine and linseed oil. Despite this, the room had an undeniably homely air. There was a bed pushed against one wall, and a small stove against the end wall.

'Hang on a mo,' said Lucy. She picked a couple of small logs out of a basket and put them in the stove.

'Don't tell anyone I've done this,' she admonished Heather as she picked up the bottle of turpentine, poured a generous measure on top of the logs, then struck a match and tossed it into the stove. There was a sudden spurt of flames back through the top of the stove which seemed to reach momentarily almost to the ceiling, together with a very satisfactory whooshing noise as Lucy jumped back out of range and then reached forward and pushed the lid down into place.

'Naughty, I know, but it usually saves about half an hour,' she explained. Sure enough the logs were already well ablaze, and it was not long before the stove was starting to give out some warmth, as Heather discovered when Lucy pulled two chairs in front of it and gestured to her to sit down in one. As she did so, she felt her dress stick to her coldly and clammily, and she gave an involuntary shiver.

'Hi, we'd better get out of these wet things,' said Lucy, 'or we'll catch our deaths. Hang on a minute.'

She left the room only to reappear almost immediately with two army greatcoats and two clothes hangers.

'We use these as dressing gowns,' she said with a smile. 'Not very elegant, I know, but they do the job. It gets very cold here in the winter, and these were only a bob each in an army surplus store. Here, let's take our things off and dry them in front of the stove.'

In the space of no more than about ten seconds Lucy had peeled off every stitch of clothing, slipped them on to a hanger, hung the hanger on a line which was obviously stretched permanently beside the stove for this very purpose, wrapped herself in a greatcoat and curled up in one of the chairs. Hesitantly, Heather followed suit. While she did so, Lucy reached out and put a kettle on top of the stove.

'We'll have tea when the water boils,' she said, 'and maybe a drop of rum in it into the bargain. I'm freezing.' She hugged herself and shivered theatrically.

'Here!' She grabbed Heather's arm and pulled her down to sit on the bed. Then, with both of them sitting on it with their backs against the wall, she wrapped a blanket around them both.

'It's awful here on the coast when it suddenly starts raining at this time of year,' she said. 'In the space of a few minutes you go from a perfectly warm summer day to something that feels more like the middle of winter, and you're chilled to the bone. I don't think I'll ever get used to it. Maybe it's the influence of the marshes or something.'

Heather was cold too, but it was amazing how quickly the stove heated the room, or maybe it was the effect of the navy rum which

Lucy produced from under the sink in a plain bottle with no label. The rain showed no signs of easing, but as they chatted both women felt the world becoming a more bearable place once again.

'Where is Miss Coles, then?' Heather enquired some time later, clasping a second mug of tea and rum.

'She went off to the marshes to do some sketching,' said Lucy. 'She'll have gone to shelter in the tram shed. She always does. In fact I suspect she might actually have lived there for a bit before she bought this place. By the way, what was so urgent that you had to run out even knowing you were likely to get caught in the rain?'

'Oh, it's all very silly, really,' said Heather with an embarrassed air. 'I was looking for mustard oil.'

'Mustard oil? What's that when it's at home?'

'There, you see, that's exactly what everyone has said when I've asked for it. Apparently it's something people use for a massage in India, particularly in the afternoon after lunch. Major Flint was telling me all about his time in India, and it cropped up in conversation quite a few times.'

'Naughty old Benjy!' cried Lucy delightedly. 'Still, you have to admire the old devil's style.'

Heather laughed, but then shook her head as if in reproof and looked rather sad.

'He's really a very nice man once you get used to his little ways,' she said, 'but very lonely, I think.'

'You're probably right,' said Lucy, which was generous considering that only a few nights previously he had threatened to take a horsewhip to her and Irene, and she had been forced to knock him down in the road. 'So, you went out looking for mustard oil, but didn't have any luck?'

'No, but I did find something else,' said Heather. 'Gosh, I've no idea why I'm telling anyone about all this, but I feel almost as though I've known you a long time, isn't that strange?'

'Oh, don't worry about that,' said Lucy as she reached again for the rum bottle. 'Everyone seems to think of me as an honorary sister or something. You've no idea the things I've heard in my time.'

'Well, anyway,' continued Heather, 'the poor lamb also mentioned sesame oil the other day. Apparently some maharajah whose life he once saved used to do something naughty with it in his harem – or should that be *with* his harem?'

'Really? What?' demanded Lucy.

'I'm not exactly sure. He just said, "The only limit is the imagination," and gave that wink he does, with one finger tapping the side of his nose. Nice smell, though – here, have a sniff.'

She pulled the bottle out of her bag and passed it to Lucy, who unscrewed the cap, rubbed some on to the back of her hand, and lifted it to her nose.

'Mmmm, dreamy,' she said approvingly.

She started to pass the bottle back to Heather but suddenly stopped, put her hand on the other woman's arm, and stared at her intently.

'I say,' she said, and suddenly her voice was that of a little girl asking her mother urgently but nervously if she could take a stray puppy home with her. 'I say, could we try it, do you think? I've really got a jolly good imagination.'

So it was that after the rain had finally eased off Major Flint came home in choleric mood after imbibing a significant amount of Scotch whisky, all as correctly predicted by Lucy, to the pleasant aroma of sesame oil. The combined influence of these two infusions, and the calming presence of Heather Gillespie, was such that, shortly before her tea party was due to commence, Miss Mapp received a note from the Major, hand-delivered by Mrs Gillespie, begging to be excused and explaining that prolonged exposure to the morning's rain had brought on an attack of swamp fever, to which he had been a martyr for many years.

Miss Mapp was initially mildly irritated by the news, but then this was her normal reaction to any news, and she quickly cheered up when she realised that this would be one less guest to stretch to when dividing up the cake. The Wyses had already sent their apologies as they were motoring over to some acquaintances at Romney, and so it was that only Diva, Quaint Irene and the Bartletts attended the event which was to pass into Tilling folklore simply as 'Mapp's chocolate cake'.

When all were assembled, Withers placed the cake on the table, saying simply, 'Your chocolate cake, madam.' Diva gazed at it, aghast. Surely it couldn't be? But no, Elizabeth had clearly said that she had baked it herself from the same recipe. The Padre had plainly remembered this, too.

'So this is yon famous recipe from the library?' he queried. 'Now, tell me, Mistress Mapp, was it a difficult one to execute?'

'No, on the contrary, quite easy, really,' replied Miss Mapp briskly. 'All you need to follow a recipe is a little intelligence and common sense, I find. Now then, let me slice it so you can all try it.'

She cut into the cake and immediately a dull metallic clang issued forth. There was silence as everyone looked at each other in total mystification. Suddenly Diva realised what must have happened (though she couldn't imagine how, or why), and glanced quickly upwards to give thanks. Elizabeth had by some divine intervention entered into a city with gates and bars, and been delivered into her hands.

Miss Mapp was of course just as mystified as her guests, and made a couple of tentative stabs at the centre of the cake, both of which led merely to a repeat of the original sound. However, patience was not one of her virtues, and she quickly started scraping away the top layer of cake, which promptly fell apart to reveal the rounded perfection of a tin of black Cherry Blossom shoe polish. Miss Mapp stared at it in total incomprehension. Evie Bartlett squeaked uncertainly. The Padre's jaw dropped. Quaint Irene's tea cup hung in mid-air, arrested on its way back to its saucer.

Elizabeth Mapp's eyes slowly lost their glazed expression and began to fill with horror. They rose slowly to meet those of Godiva Plaistow, who was attempting a look of calm equanimity, but, honest woman that she was, could not restrain a gleam of triumph. Having blanched with horror, Miss Mapp's face now began to colour with rage. Diva had tricked her. She could not conceive of how or why, but Diva had tricked her and she was caught. Having boasted of her prowess in making the cake she could hardly now contradict herself and claim that it had in fact been baked by Diva, and even if she did, who would believe her?

'What on earth is it?' asked the Padre in his rarely heard normal Edgbaston tones after what seemed like a very long time, but was probably only about twenty seconds.

'Secret ingredient perhaps?' asked Diva brightly. 'Like the jam.'

'Good God, Mapp, no wonder you make everybody ill if you go around putting shoe polish in things,' said Irene. 'Hasn't anyone told you it's poisonous?'

'Oh, Kenneth, the hospital ...' gasped Evie, staring at Miss Mapp incredulously, 'they said they couldn't understand it ...'

Miss Mapp tried to work her jaw, but could find no words suitable for the occasion.

'Perhaps the recipe called for black cherry, and you got confused, Elizabeth?' asked Diva innocently.

'Confused, woman?' echoed Irene. 'How could anyone confuse black cherry with black Cherry Blossom shoe polish?'

'Might happen if you're not used to following recipes I suppose,' mused Diva. 'Though not if you used a little intelligence and common sense,' she added viciously.

Miss Mapp tried to form several words in succession, her Adam's apple rising and falling rapidly, but failed in each attempt.

'Perhaps you're word blind, or whatever it's called, Mapp?' suggested Irene, who was beginning to enjoy the situation almost as much as Diva. 'Can't read recipes and labels properly, that sort of thing?'

'Like confusing "marrow" with "greengage" and so forth?' proffered Diva. 'Yes, that might explain it. Always wondered about that, Elizabeth. How you came to mix up the two, I mean.'

Diva could not remember ever having felt such total exultation flowing through her. Her face was hot and her cheeks were red. Both her legs were trembling violently, making her heels jump up and down off the floor. A pulse was beating strongly at the side of her forehead and she began to fear that she might be so overcome with pleasurable excitement as to have some sort of seizure. The curious sensation she had felt recently when having her thigh massaged vigorously by an Anglican clergyman came quickly to mind and was just as swiftly banished, and with it, though neither appreciated it at the time, vanished any hopes that the Reverend Theophilus Oates might ever have entertained of capturing Diva Plaistow's affections.

A lesser soul than Miss Mapp might have attempted some explanation of the situation. Major Flint, for example, might have cited the malign influence of an Indian fakir whom he had once crossed in Rawalpindi, to the dismay of his sepoys, who had been convinced of the man's supernatural powers. This might have led into an exposition on the Indian rope trick and snake charming, perhaps with a lengthy diversion into the particularly venomous nature of the hooded cobra. Miss Mapp was made of sterner stuff, however. She rose, crossed the room majestically and rang for Withers. She gazed with a determinedly absent expression out of the window until her summons was answered.

'Withers,' she said calmly, 'please take the cake away. I fear someone has tampered with it. Bring some biscuits instead.'

'Very good, madam,' said Withers, and did as she was bid.

'Tampered?' cried Quaint Irene, who was beginning to resemble a parrot, thought Miss Mapp, repeating what everybody said in this ridiculous fashion. 'Tampered? Who on earth would tamper with a cake?'

The Padre, who was secretly enjoying this episode as much as anyone, though he was of course just as bemused as Irene, decided that the time may have come to ease Miss Mapp's embarrassment and suggested that perhaps one of those wee rascals from the school might have popped in one day when the door had been left open.

Diva was about to say, 'No, that's not it at all!' and launch into a full explanation of how Elizabeth had taken her cake and passed it off as her own, when she noticed Miss Mapp gazing steadfastly at her. Silent yet total communication flashed between them. She had it in her power to complete Elizabeth's discomfiture. Indeed, she had it in her power to humiliate her so thoroughly that normal social intercourse in Tilling could become all but impossible for many weeks, if not months. She knew this, and Miss Mapp knew it too. And yet ...

Yet if she did so, she could not avoid admitting that she had entered a cake into the Spring Show which was specifically constructed to deceive judge and casual onlooker alike. If she did so, she would upset Tilling's bridge arrangements for the foreseeable future, indeed perhaps prevent bridge from taking place at all, for Major Flint would undoubtedly side with Miss Mapp and refuse to attend any event to which she was not invited, or felt unable to favour with her presence. These were indeed considerations that should weight heavily against the sort of full disclosure which Diva was contemplating. And on the other hand ...

On the other hand, if she kept quiet then Miss Mapp would know that Diva had been seized of an opportunity to destroy her, and yet had forborne to exercise it. She would enjoy an overwhelming moral superiority that would surely keep Elizabeth Mapp firmly in her place for some time to come. Whenever Elizabeth launched into one of her petty and vindictive tirades, the simple mention of 'chocolate cake' coupled with a stern glance would suffice to quell her. Diva agonised over two equally delicious outcomes, but came to the view that revenge is a dish best eaten cold. She said nothing. She took a biscuit and ate it. It was stale. How typical of Elizabeth! She had probably bought it from the 'reduced to clear' pile in Twemlow's while nobody was looking. She tried to look contemptuous and eat a biscuit at the same time. This turned out to be a mistake, as she simply looked as though she was wincing.

'Toothache, dear?' enquired Miss Mapp solicitously. 'Have them out, I should. Much the best thing at your age.'

Now of course Diva bitterly regretted her sudden attack of clemency, but it was too late; the moment had passed.

'Biscuit stale, that's all,' telegraphed Diva furiously. 'Still, better than the cake, I'll be bound.'

She could not help thinking that this was a rather lame riposte. Had Mr Wyse been present he might have conjectured that the previous twenty minutes had resembled a game of chess in which Miss Mapp had been staring checkmate in the face but had somehow managed to gain tempo, and was now even threatening to seize the initiative. However, he was not present, and all Diva could think of to help compose herself was that she would at least have the privilege of spreading the story of Miss Mapp's chocolate cake around the rest of Tilling society. Provided she could be the first to do so, of course. She shot a darkly suspicious glance at the Padre, who had just ostentatiously removed his watch from his fob and looked meaningfully first at it and then at the wee wifie. When would the Wyses return? Surely not yet, but perhaps the Bartletts were planning to leave a note for them asking them to drop in for sherry on their return? This could not be allowed. As the prime cause of Miss Mapp's discomfiture, though nobody could be allowed to know this of course, it was for her to reap the glory of spreading this glorious news, and nobody else. She stood up abruptly.

'Elizabeth, dear,' she said, 'enjoyable though this afternoon has been,' ('and I never said a truer thing,' she thought exultantly), 'I fear I must draw it to a close, at least for myself. I seem to remember that I have left a cake in the oven.'

This was a low blow, but Miss Mapp was equal to it.

'Indeed, dear?' she enquired. 'Then let us hope that it has not suffered any mishap.'

'Oh, it should be all right,' said Diva airily, 'unless someone has turned the oven up, of course.'

The Padre began to cough violently at this point, doubtless having suffered a biscuit crumb go down the wrong way. While he recovered, Diva gathered up her hat. As Withers opened the front door for her, she had a sudden brainwave.

'Do let me know if you need to borrow any boot polish, Withers,' she announced graciously. 'I fear Miss Mapp may have used yours up inadvertently.'

There were those, when this story was told and retold endlessly with many embellishments in the long winter evenings to come, who believed this represented Diva Plaistow's finest hour, but at the time Withers simply said 'Very good, madam' and closed the door behind her, while the poor Padre suffered an immediate recurrence of his coughing fit. However, by hand and eye gestures he managed to convey in succession, while going increasingly red in the face, the sad necessity of leaving, gratitude for Miss Mapp's hospitality and sorrow at contributing to the breaking up of the gathering. A final stab of the finger straight upwards suggested an urgent summons to some spiritual duty, perhaps connected with next Sunday's sermon.

The Bartletts having departed, Quaint Irene rose to follow them.

'Well, thanks for my tea, Mapp,' she said. 'By the way, what happened to the old Benjy-wenjy? I thought he was supposed to be here.'

Miss Mapp soundlessly took the Major's letter off the hall table and passed it to her to read. As Irene pulled the letter from the envelope, a very fixed expression came over her face. Slowly she raised both letter and envelope to her nose and sniffed deeply. The fixed expression slowly vanished, to be replaced by a look of pure anguish such as Miss Mapp had never seen on anyone's face before. Irene could not have appeared more unhappy had she just been told that some very dear relative had been horribly mangled in a train crash.

'Mapp,' she said extremely calmly, unnaturally calmly, 'do you know what this smell is?'

'No, I don't,' admitted Miss Mapp, 'but I did notice it when that Gillespie woman brought the note. It seems vaguely oriental, but I can't place it.'

Irene slowly and deliberately returned the letter to its envelope and then the envelope to the hall table.

'When I got home today,' she said, still very calmly, 'I was soaked through from the rain so I decided to have a hot bath. When I put on my dressing gown while the bath was running – well, it's not a dressing gown really, but that doesn't matter – I could smell this, whatever it is, very strongly. Whoever had been wearing it must have had this stuff smeared all over them. I took it off and put on Lucy's, only to discover that it smelled exactly the same.'

Miss Mapp stared at her in blank incomprehension.

'Well, don't you see?' cried Irene, with sudden desperate animation. 'Don't you see, Mapp? Two people had been in Taormina, two people with no clothes on, which is why they had needed to wear dressing gowns, and both smeared with this oriental stuff. One was Lucy, and now I know who the other must have been.'

'No!' cried Miss Mapp. 'Don't say it! Anyway, I shan't believe it!'

'But don't you see, you must believe it,' cried Irene, seizing her wrists and staring straight into her face. 'You have the evidence on your own hall table. That old goat Benjy and my Lucy have been together this morning in Taormina – very much together – and he even had the nerve to wear my dressing gown. No wonder he didn't come this afternoon. Couldn't face me, I suppose, worried I might have found out, perhaps.'

'Oh, it's not possible,' said Miss Mapp. 'I can't believe it of Major Flint.' Yet in her heart of hearts she knew that it was indeed possible, and could be believed of Major Flint only too easily.

'Lucy must have arranged to meet him this morning because she knew I would be out most of the day,' mused Irene, thinking quickly. 'He must have pretended to go to the links but got the next tram straight back, or maybe he never went at all. Oh, how could I have been so blind? I've seen the way he looks at her so many times.'

So, she had to admit, had Miss Mapp. Following so hard upon the heels of the great chocolate cake mystery, she felt that her world was suddenly falling apart in the space of a single afternoon, and she struggled to preserve her equanimity.

'Irene, dear,' she said distractedly, 'I agree that things look very black. I agree that the evidence appears very compelling. But let us be sensible. Let us at least wait until you have had a chance to speak to Lucy.'

'Oh, I'll speak to her all right,' said Irene grimly, 'and you'd better hope that I don't see old Major Bluebeard first, or I'm likely to biff him very hard on his silly old red nose.'

Chapter 9

Knowing nothing of the scandalous drama that was unfolding behind her at Mallards, Diva Plaistow rushed home to Wasters and furiously scribbled a note to the Wyses informing them that she had news of the utmost importance to transmit to them urgently, and asking them to call on her without delay on their return. This she took round and handed to their housemaid in person, but on her return journey who should she see coming in the opposite direction but the Bartletts, who turned aside and walked very determinedly towards Hopkins the fishmonger. She noted with alarm that Evie seemed to be carrying what looked suspiciously like an envelope and that she seemed to have no interest either in entrusting it to the postbox or in taking it into the post office in search of a stamp. Perhaps she should have noted the time on her own missive so that the Wyses would be clear which they had received first. Alas, it was too late for that now, but she brightened as she realised that presumably their maid would be able to inform them of the chronological order in which their afternoon post had been received.

In the event she need not have worried because it was well after eleven that night when the beam of their headlights passed across Diva's bedroom ceiling, and clearly far too late at night to go calling, no matter how important the news or how urgent the impetus. However, early the next morning the Wyses' chauffeur arrived with a note expressing profuse and courtly apologies for having returned unexpectedly late the previous evening, and inviting Mrs Plaistow to morning coffee. Diva's heart leapt, but then subsided again somewhat as she read the last paragraph, which conveyed the writer's intention also to invite the Bartletts, and trusted that this would not inconvenience Mrs Plaistow in the imparting of her news. In the circumstances she could hardly object, so she sent word that she would arrive as bidden at half past ten.

Needless to say, the Wyses were all agog. In fact the Contessa had been all for inviting Diva round for breakfast and, though supported by Isabel, had been firmly rebuffed by Mr Wyse who, despite a meaningful glance at the fire tongs from his sister, had stood firm and insisted that polite society in Tilling did not entertain each other for breakfast. To be fair, even morning coffee was extremely rare; afternoon tea was generally recognised as the appropriate time for social intercourse. It was plain that they could hardly wait for Diva to be seated before she was urged to 'spill the beans, sister' by Isabel, who had been reading an American detective story. Mr Wyse winced, Susan Wyse tutted and Amelia said 'Hear, hear', while inserting a cigarette into her holder.

So Diva duly spilled the beans and everybody gratifyingly gasped and said 'No!' in all the appropriate places. Then the Bartletts arrived and told much the same story all over again, though not nearly as effectively in Diva's opinion. Despite having had the advantage of hearing the story twice over, Mr Wyse still looked extremely puzzled.

'But why, or rather how, or perhaps I mean why after all,' he quavered, 'I mean, what on earth was a tin of shoe polish doing in the cake?'

'We've been thinking about it all night,' said Evie, 'and we can't work it out for the life of us.'

Everyone stared at each other with raised eyebrows but even that inveterate solver of crossword puzzles, Algernon Wyse, was completely at a loss.

Perhaps it was the presence of the Padre, but Diva suddenly felt an overwhelming need to confess.

'Actually ...' she said, and everyone looked at her.

Actually,' she faltered, 'I think I have some idea of how it happened, although I still don't understand all the details.'

'Oh, *do* tell,' urged Isabel breathlessly.

Diva paused again, looked at the Padre, and then down at her hands in her lap.

'Doesn't show me in a very good light, I'm afraid.'

'I'm sure in the circumstances ...' murmured Mr Wyse, glancing at the Padre.

'Aye, I dare say, I dare say,' Mr Bartlett replied, soothingly but non-committally.

'Well, it was like this,' said Diva. 'I ended up making my cake very much at the last moment – in fact, on the morning of the show, just a few hours before, and it was a disaster. Would have tasted all right, I suppose, but the consistency was all wrong. The middle of it just collapsed completely.

'Question was,' she continued, having taken a sip of tea, and glancing uncertainly around the room, 'what was I to do?'

'Indeed,' murmured Mr Wyse, giving the impression for all the world that collapsing chocolate cakes were a trial with which he personally had to deal on a regular basis. However, he was looking no less puzzled.

'I knew Elizabeth was going to enter something, though I didn't know what – still don't, for that matter. Apparently it was bought by Major Flint as soon as the show opened and whisked away. Anyway – and this is where I went astray, I'm afraid, Padre – I decided to patch it up as best I could. So I put a tin of boot polish in the middle, and smoothed a bit of cake and lots of icing sugar on top. Then I took it to the church hall, but went straight round to Irene; she wasn't in, of course, so I got Lucy instead, got her to buy the cake, that is.'

Diva stopped for the simple reason that she had run out of breath, but as she gasped for a fresh supply of air the Contessa cut in.

'Got her to buy the cake? I don't understand. I thought you just said you had already taken it to the church hall?'

'Yes, I had, but I got Lucy to promise to be at the show when it opened and buy it for me straightaway. Buy it, take it home and throw it away. That's what I don't understand, you see. I know how the shoe polish got into the cake, but I don't understand how the cake got out of Lucy's dustbin and into Mallards' living room.'

Realisation was slowly dawning on Mr Wyse, who was of course the only person in the room who held the key to the mystery.

'Mrs Plaistow,' he said slowly, 'do I understand you to be saying that you baked a chocolate cake and entered it in the Spring Show?'

'Yes, of course,' said Diva, with some asperity. 'Haven't I just said so?'

'Indeed you have,' said Mr Wyse, 'but I just want to be quite sure that I understand the situation, because I fear there has been dirty work at the crossroads and I do not wish to apportion blame unfairly.'

He paused, got up, crossed the room and gazed out of the window. This was all most vexing, and the Contessa said, 'Oh, do come on, Algy,' sounding even crosser than she usually did when she addressed her brother.

'I'm sorry,' apologised Mr Wyse, as if awoken from a train of very deep thought indeed, and Diva was reminded of Sherlock Holmes emerging from a reverie of meditation to announce the name of the murderer.

'You see,' he explained, 'when I went to judge the cakes before the show opened they all had little name flags in them and one of them, Mrs Plaistow, had your own name upon it.'

'Yes, I know,' said Diva. 'I put it there myself.'

'But,' said Mr Wyse, surrendering himself to the moment of revelation, 'your name was not upon the chocolate cake as you have just stated, but upon a white iced cake, and, if I may say so, a very badly iced cake.'

135

Diva stared at him blankly. 'But that's impossible,' she asserted. 'My cake was the chocolate cake, and I put my name flag on it myself.'

'Well now,' mused the Padre, who evidently also read Sir Arthur Conan Doyle. 'If we eliminate the impossible then whatever remains, no matter how unlikely it may be, must be the truth.'

'Precisely!' said Mr Wyse with a little bow to the Padre, and presumably to Conan Doyle.

'Well, if Diva put her name on the chocolate cake, but when you went round to the church hall it was on a different cake altogether ...' began Susan, and then stopped, looking very confused.

'... somebody must have swapped the names around after she left the hall but before Algy arrived!' finished the Contessa triumphantly.

'But why would anyone wish to do such a thing?' asked Evie Bartlett. 'I mean, what would they have to gain?'

'One can only conjecture,' began Mr Wyse reluctantly, 'that somebody was perhaps ashamed of their own efforts and wanted to take credit for Mrs Plaistow's fine-looking chocolate cake instead.'

This time it was Diva's turn to receive a little bow as the chocolate cake was mentioned.

'Oh, but surely,' gasped Evie, 'surely nobody in Tilling would do such a thing?'

'Mmm,' said Mr Wyse, very irritatingly indeed.

'Algernon,' said the Contessa, staring at her brother very hard, 'whose name was on the chocolate cake?'

'I fear,' he admitted, 'that it was Miss Mapp's.'

'That woman!' hissed the Contessa. 'I knew it! I just knew it had to be her, up to her tricks! What else do you know, Algy? Out with it!'

'For the sake of completeness, I should mention,' Mr Wyse admitted, 'that she was just leaving the hall as I entered it. Indeed she was at the cake table itself when I first opened the door. And ...' he paused to gather his strength before the final revelation, '... she was alone in the room.'

Diva said 'Oh!' several times in succession, each time sounding progressively angrier. Susan Wyse tutted. Evie Bartlett stared at her husband in horror, as though bemoaning the lack of Christian morals in the local community. Amelia made a noise that sounded like 'Tcha!' On Mr Wyse's face, distress at being the source of such unpleasant disclosures battled with his normal serenity of countenance.

Isabel was still busy making connections in her mind. 'Of course,' she cried, 'it all fits, don't you see? The Major thought the chocolate cake was Miss Mapp's so he bought it for her, and Lucy bought Miss Mapp's cake believing it was Mrs Plaistow's and threw it away.'

'So Miss Mapp,' said Susan, with everything suddenly falling into place, 'was left with a chocolate cake which nobody except Diva would know she hadn't baked herself, and even Diva could be fooled – sorry dear, I mean "deceived", of course – by some cock-and-bull story about having copied out the same recipe in the library.'

'Whereas in fact the odious woman was lying through her teeth,' said Amelia sharply, 'and deliberately pretending to have baked the damn thing herself. Well, justice has been served. I'm so glad she got her comeuppance. Ha! Algy, I feel like drinking champagne and dancing on the table! This is the best thing I've heard in years. With a bit of luck she won't dare to show her face in the street for the rest of the summer, and we can all have some peace.'

'Charity, Contessa, charity,' murmured the Padre. 'To err is human, to forgive divine.'

'I'm not divine, I'm afraid, Padre,' said Amelia, entirely unabashed, 'and if I was Mrs Plaistow I certainly wouldn't forgive her in a month of Sundays.'

'Hear, hear,' said Isabel fervently.

However, Diva was struck by a sudden thought. It was getting very near the time when Miss Mapp usually announced that she had let Mallards for the summer, and this would in turn trigger Diva's and Irene's own letting arrangements. The guineas which she made from this very agreeable state of affairs were an important part of Diva's annual budget, and it would be most inconvenient if Miss Mapp should look elsewhere for her alternative summer accommodation, and look elsewhere she assuredly would if she and Diva were publicly at odds with each other. In fact, thought Diva, it would be just typical of her petty and vindictive nature.

'Well,' said Diva unwillingly, 'I suppose the Padre is right. We really should try to be Christian about all this. After all, she can't help being how she is.'

'Why, Mrs Plaistow,' cried Mr Wyse, 'you are an example to us all, you are indeed.' This was accompanied by a bow in her direction and a sharp glance in his sister's.

'Turn the other cheek, ye ken,' murmured the Padre, presumably in approval, though it was difficult to tell.

Amelia and Isabel were much less easily mollified. They both declared stoutly that they proposed to have nothing more to do with Miss Mapp all summer, but since the former was about to depart for Capri and the latter to stay with some friends in Switzerland, Diva felt these to be somewhat empty expressions of support, though she naturally expressed due appreciation and gratitude for them.

As she left the Wyses and walked up Porpoise Street she saw the object of such recent disapprobation walking along West Street, shopping basket in hand. She found herself deliberately hanging back, as she had no wish to put her Christian forbearance to the test quite so soon, but realised that there was no need, as Miss Mapp would be well ahead of her by the time she reached the end of the street. Unfortunately, however, she rounded the corner at her normal walking pace, only to find the stationary form of Miss Mapp almost immediately before her, and accosting Major Flint, who had presumably just emerged from his own house and was in the act of raising his hat. Seeing Diva, he immediately raised it again, and Miss Mapp turned to ascertain just whom he was saluting.

'Diva, dear,' she said with studied calmness as though the events of the previous afternoon had never occurred, 'so nice to see you. I was just about to enquire after the Major's health.'

Major Benjy looked blank for a moment, then remembered yesterday's note and tried to look a little less full of robust good health than was apparently the case.

'Ah,' he said, 'yes, well, quite a bit better, don't you know? Often like that with swamp fever, I find. Comes over a chap all at once, and then can be almost completely gone away the next morning, provided you have a hot bath and an early night.'

'Indeed?' said Miss Mapp quizzically, with her head tilted to one side in the rather dangerous way that the Major dimly recognised.

'Leaves you feeling jolly weak, of course,' he went on hurriedly. 'Course it does. Otherwise I'd never have missed out on your tea party, Miss Elizabeth, which I'm sure was delightful, as always.'

As the Major was only just leaving his house he had presumably not yet had an opportunity to hear the latest news, which naturally that morning was concerned entirely with the said tea party, and he was therefore somewhat puzzled that this comment was not better received, particularly when Diva gave a little snort and gazed meaningfully at Miss Mapp.

'That's as may be,' said Miss Mapp rather brusquely, 'but I'm glad I bumped into you, Major. You see, I happened by chance to be speaking to my doctor on the phone yesterday afternoon and so of course I mentioned my concern that a dear friend and neighbour such as yourself should have contracted swamp fever. And do you know, by the merest chance it turned out that he had an expert on swamp fever actually staying with him?'

'No!' said Diva automatically.

'Yes!' Miss Mapp enthusiastically contradicted her. 'An old university friend, I believe. He called him to the phone so I could speak to him. A charming man, simply charming.'

The Major began to feel that this might be a good time to be somewhere else, but as he was thinking of the best way to raise his hat, make some convincing excuse and slip away, Miss Mapp pressed on mercilessly.

'Couldn't think how you might have caught it, you know,' she said innocently, 'seeing as it's confined to the southern part of the United States of America. I didn't realise you had visited that part of the world, Major? New Orleans, perhaps? It's very bad around there, I understand.'

The Major conceded that he had never crossed the Atlantic, but come to think of it 'swamp fever' was simply a translation of an old Hindustani phrase which he was using, and it was quite possible that he might mean a different disease entirely. Probably did, in fact. Diva breathed a silent 'Bravo!' of admiration.

'Let us hope so, Major,' said Miss Mapp sweetly. 'The gentleman certainly asked me some very strange questions. Were you off your feed, for example?'

'Off my feed?' The Major was taken aback. 'Well, of course I was off my feed. Had no appetite at all, in fact. Just managed to force down a little beef tea.'

'I don't think it was that sort of feed he had in mind at all, Major. Oats, I think.'

'Oats?' The Major goggled incredulously. 'What does the man think I am – a horse?'

'Why yes,' replied Miss Mapp. 'You've got it exactly, Major. You see, I described you as "Major Benjy" and he assumed that was the name of a racehorse. He suggested you should be kept in your box away from other horses, as swamp fever could be very infectious.'

'But, do you mean …?' started Diva.

'Yes,' Miss Mapp said again. 'Apparently swamp fever is a horse disease, and there has never been a single recorded case of it being caught by a human. So I dare say you were right, Major, about your translation. You see, if your note had been correct then you would have made medical history. *Au reservoir.*'

With this, a final smile, and a wiggle of her fingers, she tacked away majestically towards the High Street like a galleon in full sail.

'Dear me,' said Diva a trifle awkwardly, 'that was a little unnecessary of Elizabeth, I think.'

'No, no,' said the Major emphatically, waving a hand from side to side. 'Elizabeth Mapp is a fine woman, and I won't have a word said against her – as, you might remember, various people have had occasion to note.'

He winked at Diva and laid a finger against the side of his nose. Diva decided to ignore this blatant attempt to revive his faded reputation as a duellist in defence of Miss Mapp's honour. Like most of Tilling, she strongly suspected that not even the prospect of a duel, let alone an actual confrontation, had ever existed save in Miss Mapp's own imagination.

'You must admit, though,' Diva said, 'that she can be very difficult at times.'

The Major reflected upon this concept for a few moments.

'I would certainly concede,' he said thoughtfully, 'that she can be very determined.'

'And very decided in her views,' suggested Diva.

'Ah,' said the Major. 'Yes, perhaps. Decided and determined.'

With this he raised his hat and slipped away, also in the direction of the High Street. As he did so, something very strange happened. Irene Coles started to come out of Taormina, saw him passing outside, said 'Oh!' in a very strange sort of voice and shut her door again with a loud bang.

Diva puzzled over this event as she walked slowly home to Wasters, but could make no sense out of it at all. Perhaps Irene had suddenly remembered that she had left the kettle on the hob?

Nobody in Tilling ever put their door on the latch during the day, so she simply pushed on the door handle to let herself in. As the door flew open (Diva was known for the forceful enthusiasm of her entrances upon Tilling's social stage), she noticed that there was a letter addressed to her lying on the door mat. She did not recognise the handwriting, nor did she receive many letters. She carried it into the living room with her, dropped it on a chair while she took off her hat in the hall, and then came back into the room to open and read it. As she did so, a faint flush came to her cheeks. It was from Mr Oates.

The letter was a model of decorum and literary style; why, it might even have been written by Mr Wyse himself. It apologised in advance for having the temerity to enter into correspondence with a single lady, confessed that their last meeting had aroused delicate yet strong feelings in the writer's heart, dared to hope that these might be reciprocated and asked if Diva might grant him permission to call upon her the following Sunday to pay his respects in person. Diva's own experience of marriage had been both brief and impulsive, and she had certainly never received such a letter from a gentleman before, though she had read plenty of stories in which such things occurred, and she dimly surmised that a situation such as this probably had a whole system of protocol and etiquette of its own. She went in search of some tea while she pondered what to do.

It was a day of written communications in Tilling, for on returning home the Major noticed firstly that Heather Gillespie was unaccountably absent and secondly that a note had been delivered from Miss Mapp asking him to tea and 'a private little word' that same afternoon. This did not sound promising coming so hard upon the heels of the swamp fever episode, but pleading illness was clearly out of the question. Major Flint feared that this was not going to be one of his better days.

He had already endured a very disturbing and somewhat puzzling event when Irene Coles had suddenly poked her head round the corner as he approached and hissed, 'You're an evil old goat,' before running away with what sounded suspiciously like a sob. Now presumably Miss Elizabeth, not content with their brief skirmish in the street, was warming to the prospect of haranguing him lengthily at her leisure. Miss Mapp's harangues were masterly constructs that stood comparison with the first movement of a Beethoven symphony.

First would come the statement of the main theme: a lecture on the moral turpitude of malingering. This, if previous experience was any guide, would probably then move straight on to the second subject (the evils of the demon drink), essay some variations on the unhappiness of living alone, recapitulate briefly both the original subjects, and then move into a triumphant coda featuring the joys of matrimony, reinforced by trumpets and timpani. Gloomily, he poured himself a stiffener.

Diva Plaistow, in the meantime, had been unable to come to any firm conclusions as to how she should frame her reply, though she had got as far as taking out a sheet of notepaper and sitting before it with her fountain pen poised, waiting for inspiration to strike. She could not even make up her mind how to frame the salutation. 'Dear Theo' sounded unspeakably familiar, but then, given the sentiments which she intended to express, perhaps this might at least afford the poor man some comfort? On the other hand, 'Dear Reverend Oates' sounded over-formal when addressed to a man who had but recently laid heavy hands (well, one hand anyway) on her thigh. She blushed at the recollection, which was in truth not entirely repugnant to her, and was then unable to think of anything sensible at all. By the time she had realised that she was unable to write the letter without third party assistance it was gone twelve, and no third party in Tilling might be called upon between twelve and three no matter how urgent the matter, nor how delicate the nature of the advice sought. So she sat down to her lamb chop and resolved to call on Susan Wyse as soon after lunch as might be decent. Susan, after all, had been married not once but twice, and would surely know what to do for the best.

So it was that three o'clock found Diva ensconced in a very deep armchair in the Wyses' living room, from which Mr Wyse had of course delicately and charmingly excused himself as soon as it had become clear that Diva had come in search of advice of a feminine nature. In any event, there were many feminine facts of life of which

Mr Wyse was blissfully unaware, and he was determined that this state of affairs should long continue.

'But Diva, dear,' said Susan after Diva had tried to explain her predicament two or three times, until it had become clear to both of them that Susan had much better read the letter for herself. 'Of course I understand your eagerness to do the right thing, but aren't we being a little, well, alarmist perhaps? The dear gentleman is only suggesting a drive by the seaside and perhaps a little tea somewhere. There is no mention of any ... proposal.'

As befitted the awesome majesty of the last word, she dropped her voice to a respectful murmur as she uttered it. This did not prevent Diva from blushing mightily.

'Oh, I know, Susan, and of course it must seem very presumptuous of me to think that it might lead to anything else, but you see Theo, the Reverend Oates, I should say, is a very ...' she searched carefully for the right word, '... enthusiastic man. Yes, that's it, enthusiastic.'

She took a bite out of a biscuit and nodded, as if in agreement with her own sentiments. Susan Wyse, however, required some clarification.

'Enthusiastic?' she queried. 'How so, exactly?'

'Oh dear.' Diva blushed again, and was beginning to regret that she had worn a pink blouse today as she was sure that it must be clashing horribly with her cheeks.

'Don't tell me if it's awkward,' said Susan quickly, seeing her distress but hoping that she would continue nonetheless, since it promised to be much more exciting than listening to Mr Wyse reading aloud the obituaries in *The Times*, which was her standard afternoon entertainment.

'Well,' ventured Diva doubtfully, 'he touched me several times when I was last with him. I mean, it could all have been accidental, of course.'

'Touched you without meaning to? Brushed against you, perhaps?'

Susan Wyse's eyes narrowed. She had very strong views on men who brushed themselves against you.

'Oh, he meant to all right,' Diva averred. 'Did it several times, in fact. What I mean is, I'm not sure whether he intended anything improper about it.'

Susan's jaw dropped.

'Diva, dear, are you serious? A vicar touches you deliberately several times and doesn't realise that it's improper? Are you sure he was an Anglican minister? It sounds much more the conduct that one might expect from a Methodist. Indeed, I believe that physical contact is almost an obsession with them. That's why they go in for all that rugby football, I assume.'

Now it was Diva's turn to look confused. She was also, it must be admitted, a trifle miffed. This was supposed to be her womanly predicament that was being discussed, and she failed to see what rugby-playing Methodists had to do with it.

'Well, it was only my thigh,' she said, all in a rush to get the word out in the open, 'and it was only one hand – his left,' she finished lamely.

Susan Wyse breathed deeply. A lesser woman might have required an immediate application of *sal volatile*, a bottle of which Miss Mapp was known to carry constantly in her handbag against exactly such an occasion.

'Dare one ask,' she enquired gravely, 'what he was doing with his right hand at the time?'

'Why, driving, of course!' cried Diva. 'What did you think he might be doing?'

Susan Wyse felt it better not to continue this line of conversation. After all, thus far she had fielded every aspect of the matter, both emotional and physical, which Diva had been able to throw at her, and had proved equal to the task.

'So, to summarise,' she said firmly, 'you believe that some more serious motive lurks behind this invitation, and you wish to nip matters in the bud now before they have a chance to develop any further?'

'Yes, that's it exactly,' said Diva delightedly. 'Why, how well you put it, Susan. I just knew you were the right person to come to for advice.'

Susan Wyse was as susceptible to flattery as anyone and she was also, as everyone in Tilling never tired of pointing out when not actually consuming her exquisite dinners and cream teas, an insufferable snob with her MBE and her fur coats, yet she was essentially a kind soul. It was, for example, generally overlooked, particularly by Miss Mapp, that her MBE had been awarded only after the expenditure of much money on new facilities for Tilling hospital (the very stomach pump which had been used on the poor Padre, for example, had been purchased as a result of Susan Wyse's munificence), and much time sitting through interminable committee meetings. The truth was that Susan could not bear the thought, much less the sight, of suffering in any fellow human being, and it was this innate goodness that now came bubbling to the surface.

'Diva,' she said, 'are you quite sure about this?'

'How do you mean?' asked Diva.

'I mean this, and forgive me for speaking plainly, but what are friends for if not for plain speaking? I mean, have you considered that if this friendship were to grow into something more, and if a proposal did eventuate, it might be the last opportunity to remarry that you encounter?'

'Hi!' exclaimed Diva indignantly.

'Oh, not that, not that,' said Susan hastily. 'I mean no disrespect to you personally, Diva, but look around you. How many men of your own age, or even anywhere near your own age, do you see? My own brother was lost on the Somme, you know. That was twelve years ago, and ...' she was about to say 'and I cry for him still', but there were limits to what one could impose upon a friend and neighbour, so she continued, '... and there were so very many like him, weren't there?'

'Yes,' said Diva quietly. 'I've never told anyone this before, Susan, not here in Tilling, I mean, but it's almost as if I was never really married anyway. Oh, I know I say that I'm a war widow, but that's not strictly true. I mean, I *was* married, of course ...'

She fell silent, feeling, with some justification, that she was not explaining things very well.

'Do go on,' Susan pressed gently.

'Well, we got married one afternoon when my fiancé was on his embarkation leave. It was all very sudden, really, we just decided that we'd rather not wait. But it all took so long to organise – the licence, and getting his colonel's consent and everything – that we ended up having the wedding on the last afternoon, just a few hours before he had to go back to France.'

She twisted her gloves in her lap and gazed fixedly at the mirror over the fireplace, as though steeling herself to continue.

'After that, nothing went right. In fact, it was all horrible. He was wounded, quite badly actually, but he survived, though he lost both his legs. He was awfully down about it all, though I could see he was trying to be brave for my sake. I told him that it made no difference to me, that I loved him and that I'd look after him, and then ...'

She broke off suddenly and her eyes filled with tears.

'What happened?' asked Susan gently.

'He died of the flu,' Diva said with false brightness. 'Wasn't that silly? Came through all that, only to die of some silly Spanish influenza the next winter.'

Susan reached across and took her hands. 'I'm so sorry, my dear,' she said, 'but then you do see what I mean, don't you? Women of our generation have so few chances to find happiness in life that we should think very carefully before rejecting them out of hand.'

'You're being very sensible, Susan, and a very good friend of course, but I'm quite determined. I know that I could never ... well, think of Theo in that way.'

So that was that, and so it was that when she returned to Wasters a little later, Diva walked not only with her resolve to reject the Reverend Oates undimmed, but with Susan Wyse's copy of *Ladies' and Gentlemen's Letters for All Occasions* tucked under her arm.

Chapter 10

Heather Gillespie had still not returned when Major Flint's departure for Mallards fell due, and he found that he minded very much indeed. There had been times recently, usually during those few reflective minutes after breakfast as he sat with his second pot of tea and waited for his inner workings to ripen to their full majestic potential, when he had fallen to musing on how very agreeable it was to have her around the place, and even to wondering if this arrangement could not perhaps be formalised and made permanent. Perhaps fortunately, things usually began to move ominously onwards and downwards before these meditations reached any firm conclusion. However, the fact was that he had grown not only accustomed to her company but also to enjoy it very much indeed, and the house felt suddenly lonely without her around. He had never noticed how very drab the living room looked, and he thought how very jolly it might be to have it redecorated. Surely Heather would be happy to proffer her advice on colour schemes and so forth?

He walked the few steps to Mallards with a heavy heart. He had no idea what lay ahead, but he had a premonition that it was unlikely to prove enjoyable. Knowing, or at least strongly suspecting, that one was about to be lectured by Miss Mapp induced a strong desire to be somewhere else a long way away. He remembered waiting outside the colonel's office to be interviewed about the little matter of the adjutant's daughter (a petty incident which various mischievous individuals, chiefly the adjutant's memsahib, had blown out of all proportion), or standing outside his headmaster's study knowing that he was about to be beaten, having been caught peering through Matron's window with a pair of Officer Training Corps' binoculars improperly borrowed from the armoury.

It really was quite intolerable that a grown man who had rendered valuable service to his country and now asked nothing more than to be allowed to settle down peacefully to enjoy the twilight, well, late afternoon perhaps, of his days, should be made to feel such trepidation. Perhaps it was time that Miss Elizabeth Mapp was made to realise that she could not go on behaving in this high-handed fashion. He might take her to one side and explain in avuncular fashion that she risked losing all her friends in Tilling if she continued to lord it over all and sundry. He might even hint broadly that only his own spirited intervention behind the scenes, his impassioned intercessions on her behalf, had prevented this from happening on a number of occasions already. Yes, by George, it was time to take a stand. He straightened his tie and pulled determinedly on the bell.

To his surprise, Miss Mapp exhibited nothing but the friendliest and sweetest of demeanours when he was shown into the living room by Withers. This by itself was sufficient to arouse his suspicions. When he was invited to take tea with her in her secret garden, this being by chance the first really warm day of the summer, suspicion hardened into certainty. It was almost unheard of for Elizabeth Mapp to invite anyone into her secret garden. It was well known that she regarded this as her *sanctum sanctorum*, a retreat from which Withers was under standing orders never to disturb her for anything less than a telegram ('or a dividend cheque,' Quaint Irene used to mutter whenever this story was told, which remark Miss Mapp would of course be sufficiently well-bred to pretend not to hear, and would pour someone another cup of tea while smiling vacantly out of the window).

'Well, this is a great honour, I must say, Miss Elizabeth,' said the Major as he followed her out of the French windows. 'I don't think I've ever seen your secret garden.'

'Have you not, Major?' asked Miss Mapp, knowing very well of course that he had not. 'Dear me, how remiss of me. Why, I thought I had invited you many times.'

Diva would doubtless have commiserated with Miss Mapp at this point that her memory should be failing her in her advancing years, and perhaps venture to steer the conversation generally in the direction of premature senility, the danger of falling down the stairs while disorientated and the desirability of moving a daybed, and possibly a commode, into the living room. The Major may possibly have briefly harboured such unworthy thoughts, but if so, he was far too seasoned a campaigner to utter them. He remembered once as a young subaltern in the Punjab firing his revolver into a hornets' nest 'just for a bit of fun', and spending the next ten days in hospital, in great discomfort and resembling a red balloon.

Miss Mapp's secret garden was a small area set within its own walled enclosure. A willow tree stood, or rather hung, in one corner. The tree was far too large for the space it occupied and Miss Mapp had once made enquiries of a firm of eminent arborealists as to the possibility of cutting it back, but the venture had not proved a success. The young man whom they sent to inspect it had at first seemed to be a very well-brought-up young gentleman in a tweed jacket, who called her 'madam' and left his hat on the hall table. However, his first reaction on seeing the willow, in place of the due reverence which Miss Mapp had expected both for the tree and for herself as its owner and protector, had been a cry of alarm, followed by urgent suggestions that it should be cut back at once as its roots must be undermining the foundations of the house. Miss Mapp's acid observation that the house did not seem to be in any danger of falling on top of them went apparently unappreciated.

A few days later an estimate for the required works arrived, the size of which made Miss Mapp very angry indeed so that she went red in the face, breathed deeply and ripped it up. She only just stopped herself from kicking the furniture, but she went out into the street and kicked a dog instead, which relieved her feelings enormously. The fact that a passing child burst spontaneously into tears at the sight was an unexpected but nonetheless welcome bonus, and she returned to her living room in a much brighter frame of mind and spent the rest of the morning composing draft replies to the estimate, which varied from the whimsical ('It was in fact only the one tree I had in mind, not the whole garden') to the richly ironic ('It is of course unfortunate that I will have to sell my house to pay to cut down the tree which apparently threatens its very existence, but perhaps such a sacrifice is worth making and should be nobly borne'), and then got irritated all over again because she could not decide which one to send.

'My word, Miss Elizabeth, what a magnificent tree,' exclaimed the Major on first entering the garden.

'Yes, isn't it?' agreed Miss Mapp. 'Of course, various uninformed people have suggested that I should cut it down, but I really can't bring myself to do it. It isn't a question of the expense, you understand, but rather the very deep feelings one has for the tree.'

'Ah, yes, of course,' said the Major, hoping to imply that he fully understood his hostess's deep-rooted sensitivities and that her name was indeed a by-word for lovers of trees all over southern England. However, it seemed that these sentiments had not after all been conveyed, as Miss Mapp continued to gaze at him in a rather quizzical manner. Clearly something else was called for.

'Indeed!' he said emphatically. 'Which really says it all,' he thought.

There was a brief hiatus while they sat down at the little table and Withers brought tea, and he took the opportunity to glance around the little enclosed space. Flower beds lined every part of it, save only for the little gate through which they had entered. These had been planted mainly with rhododendrons, which were now coming into flower and already hinting at a riot of variegated blues and purples. They were mature plants and so there was little room for anything else, but some morning glory had been allowed to grow up one wall, and two or three different clematis along the others. It was remarkable how shut off one felt in here. If it had not been for the incessant cries of the gulls circling overhead, this would have been perfect tranquillity indeed.

'I wonder if trees feel lonely?' mused Miss Mapp as she arranged the tea things on the garden table.

'Lonely? I don't think trees have feelings, do they?' replied the Major, rather surprised. 'Not those sort of feelings, anyway,' he added hastily, anxious not to offend his neighbour or her possible arboreal soulmates.

'Not like people, then?' asked Miss Mapp softly, with a meaningful gaze. Major Flint was unsure exactly what the meaningful glance might mean, but clearly it meant something, and whatever it was that it meant, he felt instinctively he would not like it.

'Ah,' he said, in what he hoped sounded like his most sensitive and understanding manner. However, Miss Mapp was not to be so easily deflected.

'I'm sure you must get lonely from time to time, for example, Major, though I'm sure you're far too brave and manly to admit it.'

'Ah,' said the Major, this time in brave and manly fashion.

'After all, Major Benjy, I'm sure you used to enjoy the company of …' she wondered whether this might be a suitable moment to introduce her new-found familiarity with Hindustani and decided against it, and so she simply said, '… your brother officers.'

'Of course,' averred the Major, 'but then things are very different out there, Miss Elizabeth. Wonderful countryside for all sorts of shooting and hunting – fishing too, if a chap knows where to look for it. Then there's polo and golf and cricket and tennis, and, oh, all sorts of things really.'

'And a social scene, naturally?'

'Absolutely. Difficult to explain really, but when British people are abroad, especially army folk, the social round is much more intense – way of keeping busy, I suppose. Dinners, teas, tennis parties, bridge afternoons, dances in the cooler months, billiards championship in the mess, all that sort of thing.'

'But the heat surely could be very tiresome?' asked Miss Mapp, checking inside her third best teapot to see if the tea was ready for pouring.

'Oh, in the summer, yes. Unbearable, Miss Elizabeth, as much as a man can do to get off the bed and walk across the parade ground. Better for the mems, of course, they usually go up into the hills. Lot of the administrators move up to summer quarters in the hills too, leaving us poor soldiers to carry on – soldier on, you might say. Ha!'

The Major smirked at his own joke and repeated 'soldier on, do you see?' to make sure that Miss Mapp appreciated it too. However, her sights seemed fixed on loftier matters.

'So much excitement for a man,' she sighed, 'only to find himself still in the prime of life' – (the Major smiled and stroked his moustache) – 'here in dull old Tilling.'

'Dull?' ejaculated the Major, aghast as only a true Tillingite could be at any aspersion being cast upon the town. 'Tilling, dull? Surely you jest, Miss Elizabeth. Why, there's bridge and shopping and golf, and all sorts of interesting people to mix with. No. I'm quite content here, I can assure you. Always have been.'

'And yet you must find that the evenings drag just a little, dear Major? All the things you have just mentioned are daytime activities, and few people in Tilling entertain in the evenings – apart from the Wyses of course, who just want to show off Susan's medal at all times of the day and night. Admit it, Major, in the evenings there can surely be little for you to do save read a book or work on those memoirs of yours, which incidentally must be coming along famously. There must be something for me to read by now, surely?'

Major Flint, whose evenings were mostly spent in either the Trader's Arms or the King's Arms, depending upon whether or not he wanted to pass any time with Mr Wyse, was unsure what to reply to this but, as he considered the problem, Miss Mapp declined to wait for the conventional courtesy of a reply and pressed on regardless.

'It's really very silly,' sighed Miss Mapp, 'that you should be sitting in your house feeling lonely in the evenings, while just a few yards away here I am in my house feeling lonely too. Don't you think so, dear Major Benjy? Silly, isn't it? Just plain silly.'

Major Flint felt a dozen alarm bells go off simultaneously in his head, and he struggled to think of an appropriate response. Alarm turned to near-panic as Elizabeth Mapp trilled 'Silly, silly, silly' like a demented budgerigar, and girlishly tweaked the cuff of his jacket.

'Ah,' he said desperately, 'yes.'

Was it possible that Miss Mapp was finally getting wise to this, his favourite form of defence? She said nothing, but simply sat on the edge of her chair and looked sweetly into his eyes, the effect marred only by her slight squint. 'Think, man, think,' he implored himself.

'Well, of course one gets lonely from time to time, dear lady,' he said, trying to sound as matter-of-fact as possible. 'But one doesn't like to complain ...'

He realised at once that this was a mistake. He had exposed a chink in his armour and his adversary would surely exploit it ruthlessly. He cursed himself. He should have said that he never felt lonely, had no time for such childish sentiments, extolled the virtues of reading and perhaps reminded her of the memoirs, to the writing of which he of course devoted most of his free evenings.

'How like you, dear brave Major Benjy,' Miss Mapp cooed and, laying two fingers along one cheek in a spontaneous pose which she had carefully practised at the window of her garden room, gazed at him with what seemed disturbingly like adoration.

A range of possible escape techniques flashed through his mind, each one increasingly desperate and each no sooner thought of than discarded in favour of its successor. He briefly contemplated a severe nosebleed, a seizure, accidentally kicking over the table, shouting 'Fire!' or explaining that he had been secretly but unhappily married some years ago and that his wife was now confined in an insane asylum in Twickenham. Perhaps kicking the table over might not be such a bad idea ... or perhaps this was the time to outflank Miss Mapp's determined advance by telling her that she was in danger of losing all her friends, and adjuring her to mend her ways in future: but unfortunately this last alternative required a level of cold courage which the Major was honest enough to admit that he simply did not possess. However, as he floundered in an agony of indecision he became aware that Miss Mapp seemed to have changed tack.

'And what about Gillespie, I wonder?'

The alarming thing was that neither Miss Mapp's posture or adoring gaze, nor her style or delivery, had changed at all in spite of this abrupt shift of subject matter. Perhaps she had been using her frequent trips to the library to study interrogation techniques.

'Eh?' ejaculated the Major, now thoroughly confused.

'Gillespie, Major. Your ... what was the word you used, now? Oh yes, "babu", that was it.'

For Major Flint, not only was this sudden introduction of what he felt to be an unnecessarily sordid and vulgar theme entirely unexpected, it was also very naughty of Miss Mapp, since of course he had never said this at all. How like a woman to twist his words so blatantly – and how very much like Miss Mapp!

'Madam,' he said stiffly, 'the word to which you allude – I shall not presume to repeat it – was used by me inadvertently to refer to someone whom I knew a long time ago. It is not in my view a word fit for female company. For my part I regret deeply that I should have employed it. May I express my great surprise and disappointment that you have seen fit to do so and, moreover, to seek to apply it to a respectable war widow whom I have come to view as a friend. I think it best that I now withdraw. Thank you for my tea.'

So saying, he rose and turned to leave. Angry though he was, he was not beyond a huge sense of relief that he had been offered such a perfect opportunity to extricate himself, his dignity intact, from this life-threatening situation. However, as so often in the past, he had underestimated Miss Mapp.

She gave a little cry of dismay and ran after him, catching him long before he had travelled the half-dozen or so steps required to make good his escape. She clasped him firmly by the arm with both hands. 'It really is a very firm and manly arm,' she thought, as she took the opportunity surreptitiously to slide both hands around his bicep. She felt a sudden faintness so that it was not entirely a dramatic artifice to half-swoon against him in such a way that he positively had to grab hold of her lest she fall to the ground.

It was well known that Miss Mapp did not frequent the picture palaces, as she held very decided views about films having an extremely deleterious effect on the moral climate, particularly amongst the working classes, who were well known to be highly susceptible to such influences, and who, in any event, surely needed little encouragement to indulge in conduct of the very basest kind imaginable. However, it was, she felt, equally understood that such views might comfortably be held in abeyance when out of sight of one's acquaintances, in Brighton perhaps, particularly as she was self-evidently not a member of the working classes, and she hoped that nobody would suggest that the barometer of her own moral climate was anything other than 'set fair'.

A few weeks previously she had been enchanted by a film in which the heroine had a particular way of fainting. Facilitated by the fact that she seemed subject to such attacks only when a man's arm was round her waist, she would slump backwards with her back delicately arched so as to achieve an elliptical backward curve, and place one arm across her forehead, the underside towards the camera and the fist lightly clenched. Her eyes would be half-open, their lashes fluttering tremulously. Miss Mapp had been so impressed by this pose that she had practised it assiduously, though she of course suffered from the lack of a man's arm and was not satisfied that she had yet achieved the necessary blink rate required to deploy the lash-trembling technique to its full potential.

It was fortunate that Major Flint's arm was indeed firm and manly, since Miss Mapp was rather more generously provided for in the waist department than was the case with many nymphs of the silver screen. There was one hair-raising moment when he was required to take the full weight of Miss Mapp as she went into her full back-arching routine, and he staggered and nearly fell. There was nothing for it but to bring his other arm into play as well, though this necessitated bending over her much more closely than perhaps would have been allowed by any cinematic censor. Since the resulting pose bore little resemblance to the one on the basis of which Miss Mapp's rehearsals had been conducted, it was sadly understandable, nay even predictable, that as her right arm shot smartly across her face it should come into sharp contact with the Major's nose. Thus both participants achieved what they had wished for. Miss Mapp fainted spectacularly, if not entirely successfully, into the Major's arms, and he suffered a severe nosebleed.

While Miss Mapp swooned and the Major bled, Diva Plaistow was wrestling unsuccessfully with her reply to Reverend Oates's missive. Several abortive drafts lay scattered around her escritoire, each representing a fresh hope of proper and appropriate correspondence and each, alas, crumpled and abandoned in quick succession.

Even the salutation of the letter was still causing her considerable difficulty. 'Dear Reverend Oates' sounded unnecessarily formal, while 'Mr Oates' was equally so, though less overtly ecclesiastical. 'Theo', though he had earnestly entreated her to use the name, was surely too familiar and in any event might arouse false hopes in view of what she planned to say, or would like to be able to plan what to say if only she could get matters straight in her mind, in the body of the letter. The book which Susan had kindly lent her turned out to be of very limited help in this respect. The only letter which seemed even remotely to fit the situation was written by the father of a young lady to whom a gentleman had been paying attentions, to which the father took strong exception. This template began with a stern 'Sir' and proceeded to make various bellicose statements which Diva could not possibly believe to be appropriate to the present delicate situation. Anyway, she doubted that Theo belonged to a gentleman's club and strongly suspected that public horsewhipping was no longer legal.

Her attention began to wander and she started idly flicking through the pages of the book. She could not help but wonder just how much assistance it could render (it was dated some twenty years previously) to a modern lady. There was, for example, a letter to be written by a tradesman to a gentleman who owed him money, but no suggested form of response. She began to conjecture what sort of response Miss Mapp might compile, and began to essay it on her writing pad in lieu of the more serious composition which should have been occupying her attention. She was pleased with her efforts, which poured scorn on the quality of the apricots delivered the previous week, pointed out that the man's stock was flagrantly overpriced and concluded with dark hints about the multiplicity of competing establishments in the locality.

As she turned onwards she happened upon a letter which seemed strangely familiar. Where had she seen it before? She gasped, first with surprise and then with indignation, as she realised that it lay before her. The Reverend Oates had sunk so low as to seek guidance and inspiration from *Ladies' and Gentlemen's Letters for All Occasions*! In the heat of the moment it was of course natural for her to overlook the fact that she had been preparing to use this very *vade mecum* herself. She was, after all, a woman, and had, she believed, all the delicacies of her sex in ample proportion; and no woman could possibly be anything but insulted that a suitor had not thought her sufficiently special to at least compose his own *billet-doux*. At this moment, there was little that was *doux* about Godiva Plaistow's thoughts.

She turned the page again, mechanically, and suddenly a miracle occurred. There, right in front of her, was the very letter for which she had been searching. No wonder she had missed it! Instead of being listed on its own, it was appended as a reply to the suggested gentleman's missive. Clearly, she though grimly, the book had been edited by a man, and probably not even a gentleman, despite the misleading claim on the cover. She smiled a tight little smile which, had she been glancing in the mirror, she would have been horrified to note made her look remarkably like Miss Mapp. Happily she did not glance in the mirror, and so was spared this ordeal.

She drew a fresh sheet of paper towards her and began writing with a new gleam of resolution in her eyes. Carefully, she copied out the entire letter verbatim, ending with the recommended valedictory passage:

> *Theo, you have done me so much honour with your own letter that I fear this may seem a wicked and ungrateful response, but I pray that you will find a more worthy object of your affections elsewhere, and that in time we may meet again as friends when these memories are less painful to you.*

She snorted with derision as she read through this passage again. Its sentiments seemed far more charitable than those she would have been disposed to express herself. However, she duly signed the letter, folded it and addressed the envelope. A few minutes later she deposited it herself in the postbox, with the satisfaction of a job well done.

Back at Mallards some semblance of normality had been restored, provided, that is, that normality is understood to include the Major having a plug of cotton wool stuffed up each nostril. More encouragingly, however, a glass of whisky stood at his elbow. Miss Mapp felt it was the least she could do after having been the cause of his injuries, and anyway he was likely to need it after what she was about to tell him.

'Dear Major,' she cooed, 'after that unfortunate interlude perhaps I might tell you what it is I really asked you round about.'

Major Flint wriggled uncomfortably in his chair, but was aware that he had missed his chance and that there was now to be no escape.

'Fire away, Miss Elizabeth,' he said, affecting an air of bluff unconcern.

'The fact is, Major, that I must admit to having harboured dark thoughts about someone in our midst.'

She was disappointed that this startling news did not evoke any definite response. She would have expected at the very least an expression of concern to cross the Major's face. It was as well that she was unable to read his mind, as his only reaction to this statement was to think it entirely normal for her to be harbouring dark thoughts about someone.

'Ah,' he said, 'Miss Coles, no doubt?'

'Not on this occasion,' replied Miss Mapp, hoping to impart an air of mystery.

'Mrs Plaistow, then? Been some trouble about a cake, I understand?'

Miss Mapp decided that perhaps after all an air of mystery was not the best way forward.

'I refer,' she said sternly, 'to the Gillespie woman whom you have taken into your home.'

'But, Miss Elizabeth,' exclaimed the Major hotly, 'why, it was you yourself that urged me to advertise more assiduously for a new servant.'

'Yes, I know,' admitted Miss Mapp in the tone of voice of one who intends to brush aside a trifling objection.

'Why, I remember it distinctly,' continued the Major, warming to his task. 'We were standing right outside Mallards after our morning shopping, and you were kind enough to express concern about my predicament, and then you said ...'

'Yes, I know!' said Miss Mapp, much more loudly this time. 'Do listen, Major, or I shall never get finished, and I have something very important to tell you.'

The Major found himself in the grip of conflicting emotions. On the one hand he was fairly sure that he did not want to hear whatever it was that Miss Mapp had to tell him. On the other hand, she was now clearly launched into the flight-path of her peroration, and he was anxious for her to finish her endeavours and touch down again as soon as possible. While he was wrestling with this weighty paradox, Miss Mapp pressed on.

'I don't mind admitting,' she said, 'though it does show me in a somewhat un-Christian light ...' she waited for a contradiction, but when none was forthcoming she continued after only the briefest of scowls, '... but I was worried, dear Major, worried for you, I mean. You are such a kind and gentlemanly soul, but you are so inclined to believe the best of people. In fact I sometimes think of you as a sort of saint.'

Here Miss Mapp clasped her hands briefly together, as if in prayer, and gazed reverently at her friend and neighbour, who endeavoured to take a pull at his whisky in as saintly a manner as possible, so as not to disappoint her.

'Yet your virtues are at the same time your enemies,' contended Miss Mapp in a tone of voice which brooked no contradiction.

'They are?' queried the Major blankly.

'Well, of course they are,' said Miss Mapp briskly. 'And in respect of your new housekeeper, Major, I am afraid you have been sadly deceived. She is not who she claims to be, or perhaps I should say what she claims to be.'

'She's not?' echoed the Major.

'She most certainly is not,' declared Miss Mapp emphatically. 'You see, Major, I have been indulging in some detective work. I went to Brighton to visit a private detective who was recommended by my solicitor. I asked him to look into Gillespie's background very carefully. I received his report this morning.'

She broke off to pour herself some more tea, enjoying the heightening of the narrative tension that this would necessarily produce. The Major was unfortunately so flabbergasted by what he had just heard that he was temporarily unable to beg her to continue. She relented, and did so anyway.

'First he managed to track down the elusive Mrs Harrison, of whom you spoke, in St Leonard's.'

Major Flint was about to say 'I did?', but realised just in time that he was in danger of beginning to sound like a parrot, and so said nothing. Miss Mapp gave him a beetling glance from under her eyebrows and moved sternly on with the unfortunate news which it was her sad duty to impart.

'I remember that you said you had telephoned Mrs Harrison to take up a verbal reference on Gillespie,' she said, intending to spare him no possible discomfort. She was not disappointed.

'Ah,' he said uncomfortably.

'Ah indeed, Major. Your good nature getting the better of you again, no doubt. Mrs Harrison told my little man that not only had you not telephoned her, but that had you done so she would most certainly not have supplied any reference at all. Gillespie left her without giving notice, and had she not done so Mrs Harrison would have dismissed her.'

'Dismissed?' cried the Major. 'Why?'

'Oh, dear,' said Miss Mapp, and looked down demurely into her lap. 'It is so very difficult for a single woman to talk of these things ...'

'Oh, then please don't distress yourself, Miss Elizabeth,' implored the Major at once. 'I wouldn't want to see you embarrassed. Say no more.' He patted a finger against the side of his newly stuffed nose in understanding fashion.

This would never do. Miss Mapp decided that it was time for her to be brave and speak out, regardless of her tender maidenly sensibilities.

'No, I must,' she said, with a noble glance into the middle distance that could have been, and almost certainly was, copied from the Brighton Picture Palace. 'It appears that Mrs Harrison discovered some sort of liaison between Gillespie and her husband – Mrs Harrison's husband, that is. In fact, she found a very compromising note from him to Gillespie, proposing that they run away together. Somewhere abroad, naturally – I cannot believe they would have been welcome anywhere in East Sussex.'

Major Flint was beginning to resemble a man who has just been hit over the head with what is commonly and crudely known by the lower orders as a cosh, but which is referred to by their betters as a life-preserver. He managed a feeble 'Good Lord' and gazed desperately at his glass, which was, alas, now empty.

'There is more, I fear.' Rarely did Miss Mapp have such a wonderful opportunity to twist the knife in the wound, and she drove with satisfaction for the Major's vitals. 'Gillespie is not, as she claims to be, a war widow. In fact, she is not any sort of widow at all. She has a husband yet living, and the only reason he is not cohabiting with her is that he is a member of the criminal classes who is currently detained at His Majesty's pleasure in Parkhurst prison on the Isle of Wight.'

The Major positively goggled at this fresh news. Miss Mapp waited to be prompted for fresh revelations, but the Major was beyond prompting, so she prompted herself.

'Wouldn't you like to know why he is in prison?' she asked mercilessly.

The Major nodded weakly.

'He was convicted of grievous bodily harm, though apparently the judge in passing sentence said it really should have been attempted murder. He suspected a man of looking at his wife in a way of which he disapproved. Apparently he did not challenge the man, or remonstrate with him in any way, or try to find out whether there was in fact anything between him and Mrs Gillespie at all. He simply set upon him in the street and beat him to a pulp. Apparently the poor man was in hospital for six months and even now has difficulty walking. That was five years ago.'

The Major seized upon a ray of hope.

'Seven years? Then that means he will be detained for some considerable time yet.'

'Not so,' came the prompt rejoinder. 'My little man checked. Gillespie was sentenced to seven years' hard labour, but with remission for good conduct he was due for release a few days ago. Sad, don't you think, in the case of such a violent man who is clearly little better than an animal? Why, just think, he might be on his way to Tilling to renew his wife's acquaintance as we speak.'

At this dramatic juncture in the proceedings there suddenly came a heavy knock on the gate of the secret garden. The Major, his thoughts full of violent men attempting to track him down, started violently, only to fall back in his chair in relief as Withers opened the door and approached.

'Withers!' her employer chided her. 'You know never to disturb me here for anything less than a telegram.'

'Why, that's what it is, madam,' came the reply as Withers held out a silver tray with a buff post office envelope upon it.

Miss Mapp read the telegram and a gleam of avarice crept into her eyes.

'Thank you, Withers, no answer,' she said.

'Very good, madam,' acknowledged the retreating Withers.

The Major pulled himself together with difficulty and remembered his manners.

'Not bad news, I trust?' he enquired solicitously.

'Not bad news at all, Major,' responded Miss Mapp with a smile. 'In fact, hopefully very good news. Some prospective summer tenants are visiting me tomorrow.'

The Major's thoughts were, however, clearly far away from the surroundings of the secret garden. He was confused, he was alarmed, he was troubled and, what's more, he was damned thirsty. He rose to his feet.

'Perhaps this might be a convenient moment, dear lady, to thank you for my tea and depart?'

'Why of course, Major, but perhaps you are not feeling quite well?' asked Miss Mapp, and began walking with him back to the house. As they progressed across garden, terrace, living room and hall the Major conceded that he did indeed feel a little peaky, and that perhaps he would take the precaution of turning in early that night.

'Then sleep well, dear Major,' warbled Miss Mapp as she gazed after him from her front door. 'Pleasant dreams!'

Chapter 11

It may be easily understood in view of what he had just been told that Major Flint left Mallards in a state of great perturbation. He headed the short distance homewards in something of a daze, wondering how on earth he was going to broach this very delicate matter with Heather Gillespie, a lady – no, perhaps not a lady after all, he thought, but certainly a woman with whom he had but very recently been contemplating some sort of permanent living arrangement.

He found himself musing somewhat whimsically on the difference between a lady and a woman as he let himself in through his front door, and concluded that he didn't actually give a damn. For, mixed in with his natural apprehension at being the possible target of a freely roving homicidal maniac, there was a deep sadness that his feelings for Heather had clearly been misplaced. Or had they? Whatever he now knew about her that he had not known an hour or so before, she was still the same person, still the same wonderfully soft, kind, attractive woman. Was she an openly affectionate person who had formed a genuine attachment for him or was she, as Miss Mapp had hinted, a schemer who had an eye to the main chance but also, he reminded himself uncomfortably, a violent and insanely jealous husband lurking in the wings? In a word, the Major was confused.

He sank heavily into an armchair and, after a moment's reflection, called for Heather Gillespie. There was no answer. Clearly she had not yet returned from wherever it was she had gone. This was curious, since she had not asked him for any time off today. Indeed, she had given no indication of intending to go anywhere other than, possibly, to the shops. Yet she must already have been gone for some hours. He poured himself a chota peg and tried to collect his thoughts. What on earth was he going to say to the woman when she walked through the door, which she could do at any minute?

It was no good: think as he might, he could not come up even with the right opening gambit. He could hardly come straight out and say something like 'Have you stolen anyone's husband today?' or 'I hear your husband has recently been released from jail?' The drink did not seem to have helped to steady his nerves, either.

Suddenly there was a timid little knock at the door. His heart leapt. Perhaps Heather had forgotten her key? He found himself wishing very much indeed that it was her. Alas, though, the opened door revealed only a rather anxious-looking Evie Bartlett.

'No thank you, Major, I won't come in,' she said in answer to his invitation. 'I am in the middle of preparing something for Kenneth, but I just had to pop out and tell you that a very strange man has been asking for you.'

The Major felt a cold hand grip at his vitals, and experienced a sudden need to pass water.

'Looking for me?' he croaked. 'What sort of man?'

'A very nasty, rough-looking sort of fellow,' said Evie. 'And he looked as though he had been in a fight recently – his face was all covered in bruises! He came and asked after you at the vicarage, but we thought it was better to say we didn't know where you lived. We couldn't believe you really knew such a man, despite him saying several times he was a friend of yours.'

'Quite right!' hissed the Major, who felt surprisingly short of breath, as though he had been running for a bus. 'Better to be safe than sorry, what?'

'Are you all right, Major?' asked Evie in concern, as well she might, since he had turned a very unusual colour and was gripping the door frame tightly, his knuckles whitening with the effort.

'Yes, quite all right, thank you, dear lady,' he assured her, attempting one of his winning smiles, which actually came out on this occasion looking more like an uneasy smirk.

'Well, if you're quite sure …' said Evie dubiously. 'I should get back to Kenneth's supper.'

'Quite. Yes, please go, do,' babbled the Major. 'And thank you so much for letting me know,' he called after her. 'I'm sure it's nothing, really.'

This last comment was intended to reassure himself as much as Evie, but certainly failed at least in its primary intention and possibly in its secondary as well. With a gasp he closed the door, and quickly locked it. Then, after a moment's thought, he bolted it top and bottom, and applied the chain for good measure. His glance fell upon the assegai which he had purchased in Mombasa, and he propped it thoughtfully beside the door, where it would be ready to hand.

Then he walked through to the kitchen (a room which he very rarely visited) and locked and bolted the back door too. He eyed the kitchen window suspiciously. Provided Mr Gillespie was a large man (and the stories of the effectiveness of his violence suggested as much) then the Major was probably safe from that quarter. 'But what if he's not a big man at all?' he thought suddenly. Why, he had known a bantamweight in his regiment who could take on two or three large men and win. He found that he was sweating, and suddenly felt very alone.

He headed upstairs in search of ways to make the house more easily defensible. On a whim, he opened the door of Heather's room, which was on the half-landing. It felt very empty. A frown crossed his face and he went first to the wardrobe and then to the chest of drawers. Where he had expected to find the soft folds of her clothes, there was nothing but emptiness, emptiness. He stood still with the drawers pulled out, a blank look on his face.

Some time later, as the tenebrous cloak of an early summer evening was beginning to fall upon Tilling, there was another knock at the Major's door, this one much more determined than the first. After a long delay and much shuffling from inside there came the Major's muffled voice, asking in a rather agitated fashion who it was.

'It's me, and I jolly well want to talk to you!' shouted Irene Coles.

There came the sound of two bolts being drawn back and a key turned. Then the door opened to a very small extent, and Irene found herself staring down the two barrels of a shotgun which had been poked through the crack.

'Hi, look out, you clot!' she shouted in alarm. 'Is that thing loaded?'

'Yes, it is!' came the retort.

'Put it down!' cried Irene. 'I may be angry, but I'm not going to attack you.'

'Are you alone?' asked the Major.

'Yes, I jolly well am, thanks to you!' shouted Irene in a sudden fury.

'What?' came the puzzled response.

'I'm alone!' repeated Irene, and then, enunciating her words very slowly and carefully, as if talking to a child or a very elderly relative, 'Open the door and put the gun down.'

The Major seemed unconvinced. The gun disappeared and the door was opened a little wider, but clearly still on the chain. He peered around it and squinted at Irene without blinking for what seemed like a long time. Then the door closed again, the chain was taken off, and the door re-opened.

'Come in quickly!' he hissed.

Irene slipped past him into the hall as he peered nervously up and down the street before closing the door, locking and bolting it, and not forgetting to put the chain back. He motioned her into the living room, putting the shotgun back on the floor behind the front door. She noticed that a rather frightening-looking spear was propped up within easy reach beside the door and that a revolver lay menacingly on the hall table.

'What on earth is going on?' she asked, and then quickly went on: 'No, forget it, whatever it is, I don't want to know. I just want to speak to Lucy.'

'Lucy?' the Major repeated in puzzlement.

'Yes. There's no need to pretend. I know she's here,' said Irene very calmly. Then her calmness deserted her and she suddenly turned and shouted up the stairs. 'I suppose she's upstairs!'

'What on earth are you talking about?' asked a dumbfounded Major Flint.

'Oh, come on, Benjy-wenjy, I wasn't born yesterday,' Irene replied bitterly. 'Lucy's run off, all her things are gone. And it doesn't take Sherlock Holmes to work out where she's gone, either. I know the two of you have been having an affair.'

'Affair?' parroted Benjy. 'Me? With Lucy?'

'Oh, don't!' shouted Irene. 'It's hateful! Isn't it horrible enough for me with what's happened, without you having to lie about it?' So saying, she threw herself on the sofa and burst into tears, or rather great convulsive sobs which seemed to rack her whole body and were accompanied by awful gasping noises.

The Major was appalled. He had never encountered a display of such raw emotion. It was as if Irene had suddenly stripped all her clothes off and stood naked in his living room. He had no idea what to do. Mercifully, Irene's despair gradually moderated by one or two degrees on the Beaufort scale until she was weeping in a more normal fashion, but still intensely and with a dreadful hopelessness. He tried saying 'There, there' in what he fondly imagined was a sympathetic tone of voice, and when that did not seem to work he progressed to 'Dear, dear' and finally 'Now, now', feeling increasingly like Canute trying to hold back the waves. Eventually Irene was able to gasp out a few words.

'I just want to talk to her,' she managed between sobs. 'I just want to know ... know why she did it.'

'But she really isn't here,' the Major insisted desperately. 'Here, why don't you look round for yourself?'

Irene gazed at him disbelievingly, but then jumped off the sofa, pulled a none-too-clean handkerchief out of the pocket of her trousers and, snuffling into it, ran upstairs, tripping over what looked like a large metal tube on the way. It was not a large house and it took her only a few seconds to discover that the Major was telling the truth.

'Then you don't know where she is?' she asked doubtfully.

'No,' said the Major firmly.

'But the two of you have been having an affair?'

'No,' said the Major even more firmly.

'I don't believe you!' she cried, and started sobbing all over again. The Major groaned and poured himself another drink.

Irene's grief ran its course through another three cycles of despair, accusation and tears during the next hour or so, each time mercifully a little shorter than the time before, greatly helped by the Major having put a bottle of gin and a bottle of Italian vermouth in front of her halfway through the first cycle. As the shadows lengthened outside in West Street, and the level of gin diminished in the bottle, Irene settled gradually into the dull acceptance of knowing that Lucy had disappeared, that she would probably never see her again and that she would almost certainly never know why she had decided suddenly to depart.

'It's really quite ironic,' said the Major thoughtfully, having sat down beside her some time previously to help her with the gin and pass her clean handkerchiefs. 'Your Lucy has upped and disappeared, and so has my Heather. So, you could say we're both going through the same thing.'

Irene reached for the bottle and emptied the remnants into her glass, though only a few drops remained.

'I didn't know you two were ... well, you know,' she tailed off lamely.

The Major nodded sadly.

'Wonderful woman,' he murmured. 'Did incredible things with sesame oil, you know.'

'I'm sorry,' Irene mumbled ruefully, 'here I am going on like this when – hi, did you mention sesame oil?'

'Yes,' admitted the Major.

'What does it smell like?' asked Irene, suddenly sitting up very straight and staring at him very hard.

'Have a sniff yourself,' said the Major unconcernedly. 'There's a bottle open on my bedside table.'

He hauled himself off the sofa and went upstairs, returning with the promised bottle. Irene whipped off the top, poured a little on to the back of her hand, and raised it to her nose.

'No!' she gasped. 'No, no, oh no!'

She flung the bottle into the fireplace and collapsed back on to the sofa. Fortunately it did not smash, and the Major was able to swoop on it and snatch it up before too much oozed out. He felt he should be puzzled all over again, but he was growing frankly tired of not knowing what was going on.

'I suppose,' he said heavily, 'that you might, just might, be kind enough to tell me what all this is about?'

'It's Heather,' replied Irene dully. 'Lucy's run off with Heather. They've been spending time together in Taormina. I smelt this oil on the couch in my studio and on my dressing gown, and I thought it was you. But it wasn't. All the time it was Heather.'

'Good God!' said the Major reflectively. 'Well, that really does take the biscuit. Thought I'd seen everything in my time ...'

He shook his head.

'Well, we're both in the same boat, it seems,' said Irene bitterly, 'so we might as well get plastered together. Do you have any more gin?' And then, as the Major went in search of another bottle, 'I say, what *is* going on? What on earth is that thing I tripped over at the top of the stairs?'

'Elephant gun,' he said proudly. 'None finer! Nitro Express, point five seven seven. Pride of my collection. Not many of them about these days – difficult to get the bullets. Lucky I had a box stashed away. Never thought I'd have a chance to use it again.'

'Is it loaded?' asked Irene dubiously.

'Course it is. What good's a gun if it's not loaded? Let me tell you,' the Major said as he finally returned with a small amount of gin in the bottom of a long-forgotten bottle, 'that trusty old cannon may just save my life in the next twenty-four hours.'

'What *is* this?' cried Irene. 'Do you mean someone is trying to kill you? Tell all, or I'll finish your Scotch as well.'

So the Major told her his sorry tale as best he could, while Irene dutifully ejaculated 'No!' at regular intervals in tones of awed respect and delight.

It turned out that the Major's security precautions could hardly be criticised for lack of thoroughness. In addition to the service revolver on the hall table, the other half of the matched pair of shotguns whose mate had menaced her earlier stood broken but loaded, ready for action by the locked and barricaded back door in the kitchen; the elephant gun was at the head of the stairs, and beside the Major's bed lay a German automatic of sleek and sinister appearance.

'Gosh!' exclaimed Irene admiringly. 'Do you really suppose this Gillespie fellow means to kill you?'

'Miss Mapp's information certainly ran in that direction,' came the stiff response. 'What's more, the oaf is here, here in Tilling right now, looking for me.'

'No!' shouted Irene again, and the Major told her of Evie Bartlett's warning.

Unfortunately at this critical juncture a major setback occurred, as the Major ran simultaneously out of both whisky and gin.

'Hey, come on, let's go to the pub,' said Irene decisively. 'It's after opening time, and I feel like getting well and truly blotto.'

'Ah,' cautioned the Major. 'Difficult. You know, with Chummie roaming around outside somewhere …'

'Oh, bosh,' came the staunch riposte. 'He's hardly going to bump you off in full public view, is he? We'll keep our eyes peeled and if we see anyone suspicious we can ask someone to call the police. Come on, Benjy boy, you can't be a prisoner in your own house, can you?'

The Major appeared far from convinced, but after gazing at the empty whisky bottle for a while he allowed himself to be enticed out of doors. Not without taking a few precautions, however. Before he left the house he slipped his service revolver into his jacket pocket, and propped up the elephant gun ready for use just inside the front door.

Irene stared at it in amazement. 'My God, it's huge!' she exclaimed.

'So are elephants,' said the Major grimly. 'Foreheads like armour plating. Only way to get the penetration, you see, is to have such a big gun.'

'How does it work?' enquired Irene curiously.

'Simple. It's single-shot, and the bullet's already up the spout. Just thumb the safety catch off like this, and pull the trigger.'

The Major demonstrated with his thumb, though he mercifully refrained from pulling the trigger. Reassured that his favourite weapon would be in easy reach the moment he reopened his front door, he allowed himself to be cajoled along the street towards the King's Arms, though he accomplished most of the journey walking backwards so as to be able to see behind him.

Some few hours later, the Major and Quaint Irene could be seen making their way back to West Street in a somewhat erratic fashion. The Major's apprehensions appeared to have been forgotten, though it is difficult to be sure, as on leaving the public bar of the King's Arms he had spent some minutes engaging a Chelsea pensioner of somewhat diminutive stature in a one-sided conversation before Irene had pointed out that it was a postbox. He had retorted that any fool could see that, saluted the postbox gravely and continued on his way. Irene, however, remembered enough of the previous events of the day, albeit dimly, that she decided to accompany the Major to his own front door. It was to prove a wise precaution.

As the Major finally managed to insert his front door key in the lock, a nasty, rough-looking man emerged suddenly from the shadows. Attached to the nasty, rough-looking man were two equally nasty, rough-looking fists, one of which seized the Major by his lapels and slammed him up against the wall of his own house, while the other was clenched threateningly a few inches from his face, with its owner crooning 'Major Flint, I assume?' in a way which gave every indication that the remainder of the encounter was unlikely to prove a pleasant one for the bearer of that name.

Major Benjy's assailant had clearly been indulging in some reflection and meditation of his own, since his breath smelt strongly of India Pale Ale. Perhaps wafted to new heights of calm by its relaxing influence, he focused all his attention on the Major, ignoring Quaint Irene completely. As subsequent events were to demonstrate, this was to prove a fateful miscalculation.

Had Miss Mapp found herself in a similar predicament she would have screamed mightily and wondered aloud where the police were when you needed them, especially given the ruinous level of rates which local residents were called upon to pay. Irene Coles, however, was a very different animal from Elizabeth Mapp. Having finished turning the key in the lock, she reached inside Major Benjy's front door, drew forth, with some difficulty since it was very heavy, the fabled Nitro Express and managed to point it at the nasty, rough-looking man's nasty, rough-looking chest – any higher was impossible, given the weight of the weapon.

He stared at the apparition before him and uttered, in a tone of disbelief, a word which has no place in a genteel chronicle of this nature. As he did so, Irene's thumb found the safety catch and flicked it back just as she had seen Major Benjy do, and her finger pulled the trigger. At this point a lot of things happened very quickly.

The elephant gun gave forth a belch of flame and a bang which sounded like the end of the world, and rattled every window in Tilling. Irene screamed as if she was kicked in the shoulder by an invisible cart-horse and was knocked flat on her back on to the cobbles. The gun, having jerked upwards and sideways with the recoil, clattered to the ground beside her. There was a smash of breaking glass as a heavy-calibre projectile entered the bedroom window of the house of the late Captain Puffin, whom some claimed had drowned in a bowl of soup, but who had in reality most likely suffered a seizure and unfortunately fallen forwards into his soup, showing a sad lack of regard for the arcane Tilling etiquette of dying tidily and thoughtfully.

Fortunately the house, and thus the bedroom, were both empty, and the bullet proceeded on its way, unimpeded by human flesh, through first the ceiling and then the roof. As it erupted through the tiles, a pair of nesting gulls, who had been sitting immediately beside the sudden gaping hole, rose screaming into the air, followed a second later by every other seabird for miles around, their raucous cries echoing across the marshes. The sound of a dozen or so tiles sliding noisily down the incline and smashing into smithereens on the cobbles below completed the effect.

The nasty, rough-looking man remained frozen in time, with his right fist poised a few inches in front of Major Benjy's nose. His mind was clearly struggling to come to terms with his circumstances. Whatever might be the terms of reference on which he was engaged by a Hastings bookmaker to collect outstanding amounts from particularly stubborn customers, they clearly did not contemplate encounters with murderous artists equipped with heavy artillery. Discretion proved the better part of valour and he turned and ran, the sound of his steel-soled boots ringing on the cobblestones receding into the distance.

As his footsteps diminished, an opposite effect was to be observed in Major Benjy, whose courage and martial ardour now returned in full cry. Pulling the revolver from his pocket with a loud tearing sound as the hammer caught in the material, he pointed it vaguely in the direction of the retreating figure and pulled the trigger. Fortunately an instinct borne of long military experience had restrained him from loading a bullet into the first chamber under the hammer, and thus the only result was a resounding click. Those instincts now overridden by a mixture of adrenaline and whisky, the Major stared at the revolver in stupefaction, before peering down the barrel in bemusement while his thumb hovered perilously close to the trigger.

At this rather dramatic juncture, a second figure detached itself from the shadows. With a speed and nimbleness which belied his slightly portly appearance, Mr Wyse (for it was he) relieved the Major of his officer's side arm, guided him into his house and on to a sofa, came back out of the house, and then helped up a dazed Irene Coles from the ground and sent her scurrying away in the direction of Taormina. He ducked back into the house carrying the Nitro Express, which he laid gingerly on the hall floor, for he knew nothing of firearms and was not to know that it was of the single-shot variety. He closed the front door softly but swiftly behind him and with a long-suffering sigh went to attend to Major Benjy, but found him already asleep and snoring loudly, which left his good Samaritan little to do save remove his shoes and loosen his collar and tie.

Naturally by this time many people all over Tilling were peering out of their bedroom windows, trying to see what on earth was going on. However, they all made the understandable mistake of first switching on the light, so that they were able to see little but their own anxious faces reflected back at them by the window pane. By the time they had realised their mistake, crossed the room to turn off the light and crossed back to the window, Mr Wyse's speedy intervention had saved the day and West Street was empty save for broken glass, shattered roofing tiles and a strong smell of cordite, which one excitable lady was to mistake for brimstone, claiming in weeks to come that the whole incident had been nothing less than a spontaneous manifestation by Old Nick himself.

The following day, a select sub-set of Tilling society found itself invited to the Wyses' house with an urgency which amounted almost to a royal command. Miss Mapp, however, was not to be moved – literally, as it turned out. She was expecting her potential tenant and staunchly refused to quit Mallards in case the good lady might arrive early. Undeterred, Mr Wyse simply, without sacrificing in any way his usual delicacy of manners, substituted Mallards as the venue, so that Miss Mapp's property interests were protected, albeit at the unexpected and unwelcome expense of providing tea and biscuits.

A gathering which included Mr Wyse was rather like a meeting of a parliament of birds, at which, after the wise old owl has given his considered opinion on any topic, none of the other members are prepared to speak out at all for fear of being shown up as appallingly stupid. In fact, since Mr Wyse neither drank nor smoked excessively, and did not display an obsessive interest in the more curvaceous aspects of the female form, a modern and more cynical audience might well wonder if he had ever really been to university at all. However, if Mr Wyse wished to make his views clear about a matter, and this was itself something of a special occasion since he normally veered between the oblique and the downright ambiguous in his desire not to give offence by disagreeing with either party to an argument, then nobody in Tilling was prepared to gainsay him.

This was indeed a special occasion since, if truth be told, Mr Wyse, normally that most mild-mannered of men, was deeply troubled. The previous evening he too had been in the King's Arms, but his presence had not been noticed by the Major and Quaint Irene, since the latter's socialist principles prevented her from venturing into the saloon bar, so that she and the Major had ended up sitting only a few inches away from Mr Wyse on the other side of a very thin partition, and as it had been a very quiet night in both bars he had been able to hear every word they said. It was for this reason that he had decided to shadow them discreetly on their way home, and had thus been able to intervene in the proceedings to such good effect.

'You will, I am sure, have heard the disturbance in West Street last night,' he began.

Indeed they had. Miss Mapp claimed stoutly that she had heard a shot and ventured the hope that Major Benjy had not been indulging in drunken tomfoolery with his collection of guns. This placed Mr Wyse in a rather difficult position, since he had already decided that, while he devoutly wished for a satisfactory outcome to the present proceedings, he was not going to tell any lies.

'It may interest you to know,' he said quietly once the burble of comment had died down, 'that I personally witnessed what transpired.'

He raised his tea cup to give himself more time to think about exactly how he should approach this, and was greatly assisted by the babble instantly breaking out once more, with relief being expressed for his having safely survived the experience.

'I have this morning spoken with our local police inspector,' he went on, 'and have expressed very firm views indeed about the way in which local ruffians seem to think they can come into the streets of our dear little old town, play around with fireworks and throw bricks through the windows of empty houses.'

His remarks were greeted by a nonplussed silence. This was very far removed indeed from the conclusion to which most present had promptly leapt, but nobody was about to suggest that Mr Wyse might be ... er, mistaken.

'But Major Flint ...?' somebody asked, greatly daring.

'Ah, forgive me, yes, I should have mentioned that Major Flint is unable to attend this morning due to a sudden attack of dengue fever. Miss Coles similarly begs to be excused, as she has hurt her shoulder.'

'So Major Flint was not involved in any way with what happened last night?' Diva persisted.

At this Mr Wyse gave what some present could have sworn to be a wince, and simply gazed soulfully at Diva with an expression of such an exquisite combination of hurt, surprise and forbearance that she promptly answered her own question.

'No, of course not, I see that now. Just wanted to be sure I hadn't misunderstood.'

She was rewarded by a stately bow before Mr Wyse proceeded.

'Talking of Major Flint, I am afraid that something rather unfortunate seems to have occurred.'

At this everybody sat up straight in their chairs. This was more like it! So there *was* something after all!

'I have it on the very best authority that our dear Major was informed by someone whose opinion he greatly values that his life is in danger.'

The was a mixed chorus of 'What?' and 'No!' and 'Surely not?'

'Indeed.' Mr Wyse sipped gravely at his tea, with the air of a man dressed in black carrying a scythe over his shoulder. Once he was sure that his audience was indeed literally on the edge of their seats, he continued.

'Major Flint sincerely believes that the husband of his housekeeper, actually his former housekeeper to be strictly accurate, is a violent criminal with homicidal tendencies who is under the apprehension, mistaken naturally, that something of an improper nature has occurred between his wife and Major Flint, and has in consequence vowed to do him to death.'

Again the chorus of lesser birds broke out.

'And this belief of the Major's is misconceived, is it?' asked Miss Mapp intently, with a bright smile on her face.

'Entirely misconceived,' replied Mr Wyse, with the smallest degree of bow in her direction. 'I of course relayed this news to the inspector, who was greatly surprised by it as he had not been warned of any dangerous criminals being at large in the district. However, to make absolutely sure he phoned the Criminal Records Office at Scotland Yard and they confirmed that nobody named Gillespie had been convicted of any crime of violence within the last decade.'

He sipped his tea again, noting with some satisfaction that everyone except Miss Mapp was looking very confused.

'But I don't understand,' said the Padre, stating the obvious, his Scottish accent temporarily deserting him. 'If it's not true, then why would anybody tell the Major such a monstrous lie?'

'We can only guess at the identity of the person responsible and at their motives,' replied Mr Wyse blandly, his gaze fixed benignly at a point six inches above Miss Mapp's head. So abstracted was his gaze that others in the room found their own gaze being drawn inextricably to the same point.

'Whoever it was clearly behaved not just reprehensibly but extremely irresponsibly,' he opined gravely. 'Had Major Flint taken understandable precautions to preserve his own safety, then who knows what might have happened. Were a firearm to have been discharged, for example, some perfectly innocent person might have been seriously injured, or even killed.'

He deliberately allowed the ensuing silence to persist for what felt like a very long time, while the others started looking at each other with the first dim glimmerings of understanding. Miss Mapp's smile became, if anything, even brighter.

'However,' he finally went on briskly, 'fortunately nothing of that nature occurred. Though it may perhaps be for the best if we, as those to whom others look to set an example, should simply never discuss this unfortunate matter again.'

'Indeed!' beamed Miss Mapp. 'Such good counsel for us all as usual, Mr Wyse! And now I must positively shoo you all out, as I am sure dear Mrs Lucas will be here momentarily.' She very pointedly began to gather up the tea cups, although everyone knew full well that Withers would normally do that. A hint was a hint, nonetheless, and they all stood up to leave.

'I wish you the very best of luck with your endeavours, Mistress Mapp,' observed the Padre, his Scottish accent now happily restored.

'Thank you, Padre,' replied Miss Mapp. 'Yes, how well I remember her own dear house from when I visited Riseholme. Not as desirable as Mallards, of course, but very fine nonetheless.'

She ushered her guests out of the door, continuing to wax lyrical on matters leasehold.

'How I hope they will take Mallards! Not for myself, of course – why, I find the pain of being parted from my dear home almost too much to bear – but for your sake, Diva dear. I only do it for you really, so that I can take Wasters for a couple of months.'

As the guests departed *en masse*, she closed the door with a sigh of relief and went to dab lavender water on her forehead with a hand which, she noticed, was trembling.

Outside her door the party broke up, all still very much preoccupied with what Mr Wyse had told them. The Wyses headed homewards, where an excursion by Rolls Royce awaited them. The Padre and Diva ended up walking towards the High Street together, Evie having gone in the other direction to call on Quaint Irene and enquire after her shoulder.

As Diva and the Padre headed away from Mallards towards the church, they noticed a very large and very grand motor car coming towards them. As it came nearer they perceived it to be a Rolls Royce, though quite unlike the Wyses'. Whereas that was closed and sombre, impressing all with its awful majesty, this one was open to the elements, light-coloured and displaying a large expanse of gleaming metal. The impression was more of a luxury yacht, compared to the Wyses' ocean liner. While the latter could be imagined as the setting for formal dinner parties, this one's jib was of an altogether racier cut and spoke of cocktails, of continental holidays, of dancing and, above all, of fun.

The car drew level and was seen to contain a lady and gentleman in the back seat, both very elegantly dressed. The Padre raised his hat to the lady, and the gentleman raised his natty boater in reply. For a moment it seemed to Diva and the Padre that he had somehow raised a large part of his hair with it as well, and they distinctly heard him mutter 'Tarsome!' to himself as he replaced it hurriedly.

The lady leaned out of the car towards them and smiled.

'I wonder if you would be so good as to tell me …' she began, but broke off as the Padre smiled in turn, since he had already guessed what information she required.

'It'll be Miss Mapp's house you're seeking,' he said. 'Straight up the street to yon corner, and it's right there is Mistress Mapp's house.'

The lady looked puzzled, as well she might, but she waved her hand with another smile.

'Drive on, Cadman,' she commanded the chauffeur.

Then they were gone, as the solid wheels of the car rolled imposingly towards Mallards, bringing with them who knew what new adventures and excitement for the good people of Tilling.